Praise for *Man, Oh Man*

"*Man, Oh Man* is the dense cigarette smoke fog that permeates the air of a purgatory for the deeply-intelligent. A truly ontological and metaphysical experience, teeming with dozens upon dozens of happenings and un-happenings. Another way to put this: welcome to your Great American Un-Novel. *Man, Oh Man* should be added to the list of books that stand the test of time. After this, whatever Corrao writes next, please also add to that list …yes, I'm sure."

- Mike Kleine, author of *Lonely Men Club*

"A bold and innovative debut by a smart young novelist. *Man, Oh Man* is a crafty experiment of form—it's like nothing I've read before."

- Daniel Abbott, author of *The Concrete*

"Like Didi and Gogo, Laurel and Hardy or Jake and Elwood – Man and Oh Man wind and unwind; they knit and unknit … and as they do Mike Corrao's *Man, Oh Man* shifts from sweater to skein and back again. Man, Oh Man puzzles through dialogue and debate, each sentence a cog seeking to be refit into the novel's clockwork mechanism; a gear looking to connect, only to find itself lost in a Goldberg Machine."

- Derek Beaulieu, 2014-2016 Poet Laureate of Calgary

"Mike Corrao's debut is equally brief and ambitious, playing freely with language and diving into questions of philosophy, art, humanity, and being—while searching deeply into the psyche of that one guy in freshman philosophy class who's got it all figured out and can't seem to quit doling out answers. Funny in spots and necessarily grating in others, characters Man and Oh, Man plow through mountains of cold coffee and cigarette ash searching for—well, they're not sure. It's witty, smart, and unlike anything I've ever read. "

- Brooks Rexroat, author of *Thrift Store Coats*

"'Do any good novels exist?' is a question feinted in the verbal joust of Man & Oh Man, the bickering ciphers of Mike Corrao's curious debut book. It is a question Corrao cleverly evades answering, either in the book's incessant repartee—for his ciphers, in the tradition of Didi & Gogo, Rosencrantz & Guildenstern, and Bouvard & Pecuchet, do not seek answers as much as they seek to make time concrete with their voices—nor in the project of *Man, Oh Man* itself, because this is a book that is only masquerading as a novel. Much like the book of Flaubert's titular duo, it is a savage critique of knowledge and erudition. But, only in using the form of the novel could an essay of such circularity achieve the goal of embodying the nothingness of culture's inexorability."

- John Trefry, author of *Plats*

"Reading Mike Corrao's *Man, Oh Man* is like being stuck on the loading screen before the universe begins. Every half-idea, mundane absurdity, and meta-criticism is suspended and floating in a yawning vacuum, so the titular characters can examine, prod, discuss, and break the epistemologies we take for granted. Part Angela Carter, part Beckett, this novel is a fever dream in a Parisian café where the other patrons can see your existential phantoms. You look up from your chess game and out the window with a sigh, having long ago forgotten how to make sense of the chaotic outer world, and having long ago stopped caring."

- August Smith, author of *Bird Lizard House*

"*Man, Oh Man* is *Mr. Show* meets *Six Characters in Search of an Author*—funny, deep, absurd, true, good. Mike Corrao's jangled jive jazz dialogue will hold you as much as the questions the characters ask about life, the world, humanity. Seriously, just read it."

- Adam Van Winkle, author of *Abraham Anyhow*

"*Man, Oh Man* is a distorted, contemplative, and refracted look at the nature of storytelling itself. It's as if two literary critics, over-invested in the authority of Barthes, Derrida, and your other favorite literary theorists, sat down in the café of Ernest Hemingway's "A Clean, Well-Lighted Place" and discussed narrative theory all night, humorously enacting both the trivialities of theoretical discourse gone awry, but also the importances and constraints of language, the spiral they fall into both affecting their own positions as subjects to each other, to the narrative they themselves are in, and the narrative they attempt to construct with the language they weave around themselves."

- Janice Lee, author of *The Sky Isn't Blue*

Man, Oh Man is one of the smartest and funniest books I've read this year. It's a self-conscious satire on intellectualism and the post-modern novel. The author, Mike Corrao, is creative, witty, and original. His literary debut at 22 is as groundbreaking as Bret Easton Ellis's early success with *Less Than Zero*.

- Andrew Wilt, author of *Age of Agility: The New Tools for Career Success*

"Reading this book is like eavesdropping on a fascinating conversation—a conversation you must hear even though you risk being noticed the longer you listen, until, suddenly, both participants turn to you and acknowledge your faux pas. At times hilarious, meta, playful, witty, and obnoxious, most threads of the (pseudo-)intellectual debate between Man and Oh Man become what every philosophical discussion becomes if drawn out long enough: bullshit. You'll find yourself leaning in closer so you can hear what they'll say next."

- Jason Jordan, editor of *decomP magazinE*

https://orsonspublishing.com/
ISBN 978-0-9914463-1-5

Man, Oh Man
Mike Corrao

Labyrinths & Discourse

I.

Across from each other, at ease in the rigid café seating—the room empty around them, spaciously immaterial, fading into a purgatorial abstraction where their physicalities dissipated slowly and torturously—Man and Oh Man smoked out of the same ashtray, took long drags, and flicked their stubs across the table, hoping to annoy one another.

—What if there's actually a bull in the china shop?
—Then you say so.
—If I say that there's a bull in the china shop, it's a metaphor. How do I make it literal instead?
—Why would there be a bull in the china shop?
—Who's to say how things like that happen? I'm sure they do every now and then. If not, then where would the metaphor come from in the first place?
—Because bulls are clumsy and china shops are full of fragile things.
—It'd be in the second place. The bull comes to the china shop in the first place. Then someone writes it down in the second place.
—Yeah, yeah, yeah.
—Yeah, yeah, yeah, yourself.
—Maybe the bull oughta *be* the china shop instead. If you say the bull is the china shop, then who would bother to correct you? It's different enough to step away from any confusion, but close enough to stay attached to the phrase.
—I don't want to be tied to the phrase, I just wanna be a surrealist.
—Fuck off then.

Man, Oh Man continued to flick their cigarette butts at one another, not bothering to dodge them, striking the matches to light, and returning to the status quo, courtesy of long therapeutic drags, one whistling randomly formed collages of music while the other coughed into his sleeve.

—What if I want the bull to own the china shop and the whole thing to seem just mundane and typical, like this is his everyday life?
—Then don't just say there's a bull in a china shop.
—What then?
—The china shop was owned by a middle-aged bull, handed down to him by his parents.
—What if I want it to be a young bull who took the initiative to start up the shop?
—You're an ass.
—The young bull owned a china shop, which he had purchased after graduating from school.

II.

The setting floats in and out of obscurity, as if blurred by some unseen medium. Stacks of books appear, all varying in quality and edition. Man, Oh Man begin meticulously removing manuscripts from the surrounding piles. They flip through the pages, occasionally stopping, running a pair of scissors along the binding, and separating the contents. No attention is paid to the oddities that permeate throughout the space. Abstractions, sourceless shadows, static.

—If the man is annotated, do we keep him around or do we set him on fire?
—We keep the parts without the annotations.
—Can we just cut out the annotations?
—No, the whole thing is tainted once it's annotated. Imagine if you knew what Shakespeare was talking about. Just let the man talk and don't bother with the rest.
—You're increasingly and nauseatingly eccentric.
—Leave the Kenosha Kid. Take out the rest.

Man, Oh Man ran the scissors through the book, excluding the lone scene, throwing the rest into the ashtray, where they spit on the binding, and burned holes into the cover, grinning quietly and separately as they moved on to the next.

—If the book is split in half, do we keep one half entirely or do we take a piece from each half?

—In this case now, leave the second and keep the first. The poem means nothing without the analysis, so it's useless, but if we take the analysis without the poem, then we get to piece back together some literary phantom.

—What's the difference between annotations and analysis?

—The analysis is fake here. The annotations were real there.

They cut along the binding and remove that which can be salvaged. The remains are burned. Cover turning pale, curling into ashes. Name disappearing, fading into a blur. The two conversationalists move forward through the predetermined set of tasks, carrying with them a false sense of omniscience.

—What do we do if the whole thing is gibberish? Do we still have to cut it apart?

—Gibberish isn't perfect, it's just harder to critique.

—What do we take out then? The play or the prose?

—The play is part of the prose. It's not annotations or analysis. We can't treat it any differently.

—Then what?

—Cut out the middle, then toss the rest.

—Why the middle?

—Why anything else? If there's a story to walk through, we're already in the midst of it. If there isn't a story, then it doesn't matter what we cut out.

The book flopped onto the pile and loose pages began spilling out from the mouth of the binding. Page numbers emboldened by the strong wood grain. They hissed in the fire, writhing with pain as they turned to ashes, falling into the grooves of the table.

—When do we know if we've burned enough of the books?

—We won't. Our job is to do what we're compelled to do. The books will always be there, as will the scissors and the ashtray. We'll always have cigarettes to smoke and things to talk about. They'll all be here until they no longer have the reason to be.

III.

—I think a good piece of art, or specifically literature, ought to be a piece of abstract expressionism. Any other style would be deceptive and false.

—Which works are abstract expressionist? This one? I don't think so.

—Maybe it is. Who's to say?

—I'd think, if it was abstract by any means, we wouldn't be using words or language at all. If it was what you say it is, then I imagine that it'd be a bunch of jumbled chaos all thrown together, as if it meant something grand.

—Oh yeah?

—Words don't exist outside of context. They have a history, therefore they can't be abstract. The whole point of abstract images is to make things that exist outside of history and context. You want them to give off their own meaning.

—How about this: what if we forgot about the whole presentation aspect of it and instead just made something that tries not to make reference to anything? Take out the story and setting and characters. All that jazz. That might be enough.

—Why bother tying ourselves onto something? Isn't the whole project of trying to make abstract expressionist literature inherently not? We're tying ourselves to a historic moment. The whole thing needs context then. Why not just make something of yourself?

—I don't get you.

—I'm not the confusing bit here.

Man, Oh Man exchanged glares, struck by the morphing colors. Something malicious lingers around the edges of the room. They cannot place what it is right now, but they can feel that it is there, slowly approaching the center. Something uncanny in its geometry.

—If the piece doesn't have any characters, then who's telling the story?

—There isn't a story.

—Then who's speaking?

—I don't know, some narrator. Maybe it's just some disembodied voice that functions exclusively as these descriptive blocks of text. If there isn't a story or characters, then I imagine we're just watching either something or nothing happen inconsequentially.

—What's the point of that?

—Honesty in mundanity. I'm not sure.

—Entertainment?

—Is there a reason to entertain people? Why not torture them instead? Make them do something painful or horribly typical. Things should be legitimate. Stories aren't legitimate.

—What are we then?

Man, Oh Man, flickering in and out of the moment, briefly tied to images of skeletal figures and rotting wooden beds, continued to smoke, to crush their stubs against the ashtray and throw them at one another, disregarding an unconscious oddity that hung over them.

—I think we're two men, no two specifically, having a friendly discussion. What else is there to know?

—Are you curious at all about status?

—I'm not, neither are you. This is how things are. Coffee and cigarettes can only be reduced to useless speech and apathy. If you have a different endgame, you're imbecilic.

—Have you ever been so bitter?

—I've always been so bitter. I always will be so bitter.

IV.

—The bull has owned the china shop since he was twenty-two.

—That works.

—Now he's thirty-four and he wakes up to night terrors where he sees his mother making out with Marcel Duchamp and his father getting handsy with Walter Benjamin.

—Why do you do this?

—If he isn't in some kind of agony, then how can I pretend he's real?

V.

Man, Oh Man watch someone crawl onto the table. The figure curls its back and shakily lifts itself onto the wood surface. An identity materializes within the figure. Old and wheezing. George Eliot looks at the two of them and smiles, her eyes ticking back and forth between them like a metronome.

—When you wrote a book, was your goal to make the reader fall asleep, or did you want it to read more like a hand-drill in the skull?
—Do you ever have wet dreams of Mr. Deronda? Maybe back when you were in your coffin or something? Or was he alive in the coffin? I don't know the conversion rate between real and fake people.
—Mr. Deronda wasn't real. That's a secret. I don't tell people.
—We're honored to know, of course.

George, still between the two men, uncrosses her legs and slowly lowers herself off the table and down onto a seat, guiding the descent with her wobbling cane. Her eyes still move in cadence between Man, Oh Man.

—People call me George. It's not my real name. Another secret.
—You're full of secrets, Mary. None of them mean anything, and none of them have any use, but nonetheless you're still full of them. I admire that about you.
—Do you hate her or do you love her? I don't understand.
—Things can be grayer than that. I can hate the book and love the person. If your mother wrote smut, she'd still be your mother. I like the parts of her that don't make sense and hate the bits that want to be profound.
—What about as a person?
—What does that have to do with anything?
—A name is a name is a name is a name is a name is a name is a name is a name is a name is a name is a name is a name is a name is a name is a name is a name is a name is a name is a

name is a name is a name is a name is a name is a name is a name
is a name is a name is a name is a name.
—You're insightful.
—You're spiteful.

Man, Oh Man glared at one another, Mary's eyes split, catching the
passing gazes that pressed against her temples while her body
began to dissipate into the air, whether it be by way of dust and
age, or by way of the inevitable ambiguities that soak up the room.
Only combative voices remain.

—Do they serve lunch here, or is it only coffee?
—They don't serve coffee. They don't serve lunch.
—What if a young, well-to-do man like Mr. Deronda walked into
the china shop and didn't mind that it was owned by a bull?
—Then you'd have what you want.
—I don't know what I want. Maybe I want the bull to be an
outsider or I want Mr. Deronda to be a racist. Who's to say what
should come out of the whole interaction?
—It oughta be mundane.
—Mr. Deronda was such a beautiful man. He wasn't real, but still,
he was beautiful.

Man, Oh Man ignore her as she continues to disappear. Her body
is unable to hold its shape. It can no longer latch onto the table or
the conversation. George Eliot disappears into the ether, but no
one seems to notice as it happens.

—She was nice.
—Or she was trash and we didn't realize it. Sometimes I don't
know if the things we do are legitimate, or if they're just there to
waste time.
—We aren't capable of it. There's no time around here. There's
never a means to an end.
—She was nice.

The Capitalist Handstand

I.

Business attire swinging, luxury watches piling up at the base of the wrist, tie ticking like a pendulum blade, the expensive man stood on his hands atop the conference room table, face turning redder and redder as the meeting went on. Industrial images persisted outside the window. Two men sat in front of him: Man and Oh Man.

—Marx opened the spell book and let out all the ghosts!
—We've turned into some colloquial pastiche.
—Are you expecting a round of applause?
—I don't know if he expects anything. From up close, he looks just like an idiot. It's uncanny.
—I've seen all the men in the world masturbating to the commodity fetish!
—How long will it take for your head to pop from all the blood?
—I don't know, but I'm not looking forward to when it does; then we'll just be stuck with his ugly body swinging around.
—That's okay. I just want things to be quieter.

Man, Oh Man watched the businessman sway back and forth. Horns blared outside. The windows flickered in and out of sight. The glass constantly moved between visible and not; although always audible. The slight ting of the surface droned on, as it was meant to. Neither of the conversationalists paid it any mind; the businessman winced every so often from the repeated clinking.

—The world needs a new look, something relaxed and loose!
—No one asked you. Not now or in the first place.
—Leave it be. Proclamation is his agenda. He has to talk.
—No, he doesn't. His agenda is to not be here in the first place. And if he can't do that, then his agenda is to be invisible. You shouldn't even notice the guy.
—Yeah, yeah, yeah.
—If he knew how to do his fucking job, then he'd shut up.

—Hands off my daughter! Hands off my wife! Hands off the whole damn place!

—Is that the beginnings of a manifesto?

—If it is, we ought to find him a ghost writer. It sounds like trash.

—No more hands in the first place! Chop them off the newborn infant! Start anew!

Man, Oh Man watched the reddening head burst, splaying paint across the table, dripping off the edges and soaking into the carpet. The horns quieted. Man, Oh Man cracked a window, took out a cigarette, and lit the end. The carpet reached out in dense red patches. They ignored it.

—Can a ghost writer fix the entire head, or just what comes out of it?

—Only the latter, unfortunately.

—It's funny that he ends up dripping red. Who knew?

—Maybe he wanted things to end metaphorically, maybe he was repressing his feelings, or taking bribes from the wrong trenchcoat-wearing man. Who's to say?

Man, Oh Man watched the head continue to drip, saturating the carpet and drywall until they too began to drip, flooding the room with bright red paint. Cigarette smoke slowly climbed out of their mouths and into the open air.

—Marx marks the spot where Trotsky rode his horse into town, on the run from our father Joseph, who deceived his father before him.

—Are you the new prophet then? Come to fix the whole dilemma here?

—I don't know if the point is to be prophetic, but I think there are better answers than the ones we're muttering about right now.

—Yeah, yeah, yeah.

—Is that the new catchphrase?

—If it is, it'd say more about you than me. This conversation is making me nauseous. You don't say anything, you just work your way around it instead.

—It's not my head that's spilled out on the floor.

—It's not mine either.

—Maybe in some derivative way it is, and you're just sucked up in some kind of denial.

II.

—Stereotypes are the product of narrative. The reason we never get to know anyone is because we don't have time; we're too busy progressing the story.

—I don't know about that.

III.

Man, Oh Man sat across from one another, lackadaisically slouched in their seats, taking drags from one another's cigarettes, pickpocketing the next from each other's pockets, avoiding the chaos in front of them: jagged lines of yarn that, in their randomness, occasionally formed triangles.

—This doesn't mean anything.

—This is the plot. It goes from here to here and then to here and there. It ends there. You've seen it before; you know how it works; what it looks like.

—How much does it cost?

—If it just goes across in a flatline, it's ten; if it's a circle, it's thirty; if it's a triangle, it'll be a couple hundred. That's just the baseline, though. If you want the whole package, you'll have to give up your legs.

—I thought the capitalist was still soaked up in the other room.

—How many rooms are there?

—I don't know; it's either one or infinity. I hate that word. Infinity is so dramatic to say.

—It's dramatic to say because it's dramatic to think of.

—I can't tell whether you're trying to be sincere or sarcastic.

—The baseline triangle cost a million. If you want to cut off the bottom of the triangle and just turn it into a bent line, it'll be double that.
—I don't have any money. Neither do you.

Man, Oh Man patted down their pockets, then looked at one another; hands ran over the mess of yarn, knotted and untied. They checked under the table and back over it, then around their mouths. One blew the tobacco out of his cigarette and the other unrolled it between his fingers.

—What does it matter if there's any money to spend?
—We could just take the triangle; avoid the roundabout economics.
—No. The triangles are a million, the bent lines are double, the other two are ten and thirty. We can't just take these things. The table would notice.
—It's alive?
—I don't know about that. It notices things. Who knows whether or not it's alive?
—I think you might be an idiot.

IV.

Man, Oh Man remained in their seats, materializing thoughts of Warhol-made machines, arrangements that popped into view behind them, obscured over their shoulders, behind their heads. The first didn't mind, and the other didn't care.

—The only real art that exists is in factories. God bless them.
—I can't ever tell whether or not you're serious, or if you mean the things you say. They all come out the same way.
—Warhol was a failure. He neglected the fact that his installations, like the soup cans, could be done at whatever singular time. But factories live forever. Some worker comes in, supports his family, and he stacks those soup cans for eight hours a day, five days a week. It's brilliant.
—You're nauseatingly romantic.

—I've heard it before. Warhol's dreams, his parents always told him the same thing. The boy was a natural: the bourgeoisie romantic. No. Consumerist romantic? Something wealthy and poured out of a Campbell's can.

—Stop speaking at me. I can't stand it. You always project your voice as if I'm sitting somewhere over there, when I'm clearly not.

—He tried, Warhol did, to invent soup without realizing that someone else already did. He wasn't anything new, just something pretty: a stylish pastiche. Mimicry not parody; the boy was in love.

A banner fluttered between the two, flashing the words "PASTICHE! PASTICHE! PASTICHE!" in bright colors, temporarily disorienting one, while the other smacked it out of the way. Man, Oh Man resumed their roles, uncomfortable in the rigid seats, again smoking, again blowing it in one another's faces.

—It's a shame he couldn't live up to the factory. It's a shame.

—You're awfully optimistic. Tonally, I mean. It's disgusting. If I knew you were in love with the man, I would've chosen someone else to talk to.

—Could you?

—If you don't shut up, I might have to. Who's to say where you'd end up.

—Somewhere else, I hope.

—We both do.

Man, Oh Man sighed and looked away. One shook his pack of cigarettes and the other scratched at the table surface, carving his fingernails delicately into the wood. Corners of the room reproached inward, turning black, out of sight.

—The bastard didn't know that reality is mundane tasks, repeated endlessly.

—Does reality never end then?

—It's a useless question. If it ends, it ends; if it doesn't, it doesn't.

—That doesn't mean anything. You avoid conversation and just turn everything into apathetic fits of duality. I hate it.

—Whether you do or don't. I do it still.

V.

—How much did the plot cost?
—As a triangle? It was something over seven, I think. I can't remember without the yarn.

VI.

—Have you ever seen the man with soup cans in his hands?
—I've never seen it and thought it meant something.

Prophecy

I.

Man, Oh Man sat beside one another, looking across the room to the back wall of the café where a lone radio sat on the counter. The lights flickered, the dials turned back and forth, ticking and vibrating. The two leaned back in their seats and listened to the static.

—Static is the only accountable placeholder.
—It's only accountable if you have an idea of what it means. If it's always crackling and dipping out, how can it be the constant? The constant is the radio.
—The constant is the radio. The placeholder is the static.
—What's the difference?
—The constant is always there. It's the reliable bit that you can always count on. The placeholder is the thing that takes the place of the variables when they aren't reliable.
—The transitional state?
—The transitional state is the placeholder, between the variables, displayed by the constant.
—Static is gibberish.
—The gibberish is the placeholder, between the variables, displayed by the constant.
—Shut up.

Man, Oh Man continued watching the radio as it faded in and out of static. Voices slowly began to creep in from the other channels, displacing the white noise. One voice grew into something definitive and clear. The two conversationalists pulled out their cigarettes, lit them, and took a drag. The radio spoke:

II.

—I can only see the black, the lack of light, the hints of where it should be but is not, where all light has been stolen to make way for the visual silence silence silence of the air around me through which nothing moves. My eyes are melting overwhelmed by the emptiness, something cosmic in front of me I don't understand, I see it then I don't, all of the lights are gone they have been gone, I don't know how long as long as they have been and as long as they will be I'm unsure that they could return, if they wanted to they would be sucked up by all of the darkness, the black hole maybe that's what it is pulling everything inward, pulling all of the tiny particles out of reach, the photons turned off by some trickster god standing next to the switch turning everything into nothing. All I see is nothing, nothing consuming, nothing twisting around me, I'm not sure whether to say that I'm drowning or suffocating, I'm surrounded or I'm alone or I cannot speak. Every sound is deafening. The lights all gone, its language all faded away, every tip of the tongue turns into clanging machinery, every touch of noise echoes endlessly ticking against my forehead jutting sharply into my ears then bouncing off the walls again and again ricocheting back and forth back and forth on my ear drum. I must be drowning all of the ways the sound returns to me. Or maybe I'm tortured. That cosmic figure looming overhead holding up the blackening beam that umbrellas my surroundings, clicking its tongue like the hands of a clock sadistically standing above me laughing about everything that they've created for me, seemingly out of spite, churning the pot turning me green and mad. I've lost sight of my own form, unsure of where my body has gone off to, my eyes sunken out unused overwhelmed by their uselessness, I've lost my senses, they've slowly faded away from me, my arms must be gone my legs my torso my mouth has dried up terrified by the possibility of progressing the echoing noises any further, the only thing I'm certain of is my ears, tortured, forced to listen to the sounds of these clicking tongues, the choir of hellish sounds followed by silence. The brief moments of silence are beautiful and painful, I feel alone like some bum on the street sleeping in the alleyway invisible to the world around me, I'm sure whomever has forgotten about me there's no one left except me, I cannot be denied that, all that's left is me the cosmic figure the blackness. Everything else has rotted away and turned to mush, the planets must've all collided and all of the people died, maybe we're all here, making the ticking sounds and trying to find one another, empty heads floating around the emptiness bumping into one another and shouting. The world must be gone. It couldn't have lived for so long as I have as I wish I had not, I wish I could have been the world and the world could have been me but now we're in our rightful places and the universe has properly acted. I can only imagine the way things changed. They must've, not fully or in any meaningful way, yet still.

III.

Man, Oh Man listened to the static return, the murmurs grow louder, and to the voices replace themselves. They took another drag, tapped the tip against the ashtray. The radio continued:

IV.

—I must be in oblivion now turned all about and disorientated by the jarring emptiness, desperately searching for what is familiar, something of note I can only remember images not of myself, only of the things that continued on after I disappeared. The world lived for too little and I live for too long I mourn the death and envy it begging for my own disappearance, to return to nothing, to join existence as the sheet of nothingness surrounding me that bounces the echoes of sound back at me percussing insistently I beg I beg I beg the images alive left here with me in the role of some obscure archivist burdened with faint memories of history ending however long ago before me, much before me some other time. I'm so old, I'm so old I can remember my memories returning I remember them, images filed away and dug up from storage. Images colliding I remember: who now I was, maybe before maybe as I am unsure I go on and return, eclipse going and returning going and returning from pole to pole tipping the tap three times then stopping, clicking its tongue, the incessant clicking, metronome noises coming out of the mouth that hangs behind the black screen fantasy symbolic real. I can only see the real. All the fantasy screens gone deprived of reality alone with the real persons all gone, nowhere around nowhere, I am here in the nowhere, looking out to nowhere, find nothing, only visible is the nothing I remember I'm so old, I cannot remember memories fading I can't remember where they've gone, somewhere else nowhere elsewhere, giving way to the darkness, absorbing the light, I cannot remember the light, it hadn't been here before, I hadn't lost it I've lost it now I've misplaced it going in and out, moving elliptically returning to returning, I could see the world not anymore, all gone now, dead men all gone now, on my own, I remember not the dead men myself, I remember myself somewhere else nowhere that I know, somewhere else I want to be gone wrapped up in the screen again coiled in the screen, coil me in the screen all lost and strewn about, I am I am I am. Being, I remember, being I was I say I was no longer cannot find in search of, I've lost the clocks, there used to be clocks no longer, they've all flown away, floated out of the peripherals, disappeared dissipated dissolved, left me alone I remember the being I had been, no longer no longer moving as so, where have all the images gone, have they all left me alone, have I been left, am I gone, in search of, I've lost them, fearful they have they have no more being I remember the being, being I was, I say used to used to. It was me and then not no longer, what am I? Where am I? Who am I? Thoughts abandoned lost, I've lost the thoughts the images the sounds, all is the sounds, the clicking tongue that clicks clicks clicks, dissipating, echoing echoes from the peripheral I cannot find the peripheral that beats against my ear drums endlessly going going going on and on never stopped, stop I say. I beg for the end, the stopping, the clicking tongue elliptical moving no more no more, the dead men no more I remember the world so vaguely, my thoughts no longer, all gone all gone, I remember green green green green green green echoing inside of me. Where has my body gone? All of the limbs floated about somewhere or another somewhere else elsewhere away from me disconnected, I cannot feel the darkness, I can only hear, are they ever there in the first, have they tricked me, the cosmic all circling around me oh please no more no more no more all the being I remember no more I beg no more, the nothingness I remember, I remember the nothingness that I am now what I used to not be, I used to be no longer I say left behind, seduced and abandoned, where have they gone, all of the clicking tongues, all the clicking tongues cosmic end, have all of the cosmic left, have I entered the nothingness, are all of the words gone now, all of the thoughts I remember the thoughts I lost, I lost them gone forever, I cannot remember the clicking tongues, they've gone where have they gone?

V.

Man, Oh Man yawned, took another drag, and glanced at one another, absent-mindedly listening to the radio messages as they faded in and out, the voices never changing, always speaking to them in this perpetual and tired monotone. The radio turned back to static and they flicked ashes into each other's faces.

—I've grown increasingly sick of placeholders.
—It's good to break up the sounds of a poet. If you hear it all at once, you might not bother listening all the way through. If it's cut up into pieces, then you have time to digest it.
—You've turned into an absurdist.
—I'd rather be an absurdist than a realist. Look at what reality did to the bastard on the radio. He wants to be real and all it's done is tear his brain to pieces.
—I'd rather be insane than stay here.
—You say that now, but once you hop off into reality you'll start complaining about how you wish you could've been an absurdist.
—Yeah, yeah, yeah.

Man, Oh Man checked their watches, lit another cigarette, took another drag, and looked back to the radio, leaning back in their chairs, trying to find an impossible comfort. The radio voice returned:

VI.

—The clicking tongues used to tick like the old man clock the wall clock used to move its hands like a magician I remember the old man, the images of the clock man used to used to all of it dripped away disappeared under the black screen drowning on the other side myself on this side I say I cannot remember where have the images gone, my thoughts, the sounds, I remember the sounds all gone now wherever they've left to, not here not me not here they've gone away but I'm still here still drowning in the darkness, all of the light pulled away sucked into the black hole, my body moving upward and downward and whatever direction I cannot see, where have the bodies all gone, I saw them, no longer but before, I saw the bodies before me in the world, it was it says, all the way around and back then around and back spinning and spinning never stopping, until the end of being it stopped at the end and never started up again, not now or before or after. All of the bodies gone: was, is, will be; left, leaving, will leave; came, coming, will come. O prophetic soul gone away who took all the bodies dragged them away it says it came to take and leave all of the bodies floating on their own, disconnected limbs all torn off to float on their own, the digits, the eyes, the mouth, the ears all torn apart floating off in their own directions, existent envy the existent, all made of material, real as it is floating as whole: the eyes are whole, the limbs are whole, the mouth is whole, the ears are whole whole whole whole whole, the pieces are whole, the whole is not the bits all taken alone, I remember the sounds I remember the clanging metal, clicking tongues, exploding dirt, the sounds returning to, they've returned, the clicking tongues never away, never never the being of all being, what is that? The world all shredded pebbles picked apart, the images that I cannot remember, the given ones, the taken ones, matter, before, they'd been here before the cave walls no shadows now, no reflections just the darkness, everything is the black shadow where the image used to be, the image is the whole, nothing but the fantasies removed, alone now, alone with the being the cosmic the nothingness, I envy I say I wish the nothingness, I long but nothing no matter no nothing just the being, the being I remember without desire to, no desire to feel nothing but the need to escape, no more no more no men die no more, I wish to disappear where have all of the images gone, all of the cave shadows, the cave, where are we now? Where has it gone now? My own name I cannot remember myself, the things around me, the nothing that surrounds me, everything has left me behind or I it, where have all of the things of the world pooled together that is so far from me so completely out of my view away from the set of eyes, their whole that floats in the elliptical around us all that they can no longer see any of the things that used to loom around here where have they all gone I say I can only reminisce, no more memories, memories dividing I cannot remember all of the things that have disappeared that have absorbed all of the light and turned invisible cloaked by the blackness acting the cosmic way, clicking their tongues outside of my reach, taunting me like the bastard gods, the ones that cannot exist that only are the passing thoughts, the ones that I've lost, where have they gone now? The world the people the things that used to surround me that might still that cannot that contort themselves into the shapes of water which drown me unseen all of the things that I knew have left, now my own memories, faded away, the clicking tongues taunting me taut taunting where have they all gone, all gone the things that I thought of, all gone now I remember, I remember that they are no longer there, the cosmic existent laughing at me mocking me where the being has gone, I cannot see where the being has gone, where it ever was before, after the burning heat the hellish way it prods my limbs and the way it sunk my eyes in, shriveled up the whole pieces of my body and turned them into specks of dust, the cosmic bastardization, the unwed woman moving upward downward, the passing thanatos mocking the sounds of garbled voices constructing the static mounds destroying the being, the being that is detaching the bodies piece by piece, taking the smaller portions and making them wholes, the torso is whole, the legs are whole, the arms are whole, the head is whole whole whole whole whole whole whole whole whole, all but now no more, all the world, all gone now, all the dead men die no more, the thoughts passing by having passed by so long ago dragging away the ever-moving mind replacing it with the stillness, the unchanging pieces that float around circling the absorbed light all of clusters that hang down as asteroids all the many passing, passing through the thoughts I remember I've turned so old I can remember, passing through the caves the memories of the cave the ones that have abandoned me I remember.

VII.

Man, Oh Man picked up the ashtray and threw it at the radio, breaking the dials; the voice faded away completely as the static consumed it. The two conversationalists turned to face each other as the café walls darkened, and the surroundings returned to their obscured form.

—I'm tired of listening to this psychoanalyst-type bullshit.
—You said before that he was just a whining realist. Which one is it?
—Why can't it be both? Psychoanalysts can be realists, realists can be psychoanalysts. If you're an existentialist it won't affect your job as a doctor.
—It affects your job as a prophet.
—Who said anything about a prophet? The guy on the radio was just some poor bastard floating around space.
—Maybe he is, maybe he's not. Who's to say?
—Whenever you turn to dichotomies, I feel my stomach eating itself.
—If the man had nothing to talk about, yet still was forced to speak, then something prophetic is bound to come out of his mouth.
—Yeah?
—Just by way of random chance, I think, if nothing else.

Man, Oh Man nodded their heads, took a drag, and sipped the now cold coffee from their cups. The table hobbled back and forth, thrown off balance by a chipped foot. They leaned back in their chairs and ignored one another. Static faded into the white noise and everything, for a brief moment, fell silent.

Dissections

I.

Leaned up against tall concrete slabs, breathing in each other's smoke, Man and Oh Man looked out at the surrounding buildings, whose walls were covered with crude murals, layered over by muttled cinematic projections.

—There is no difference between a camera and a gun.
—I think you're an idiot.
—Either way, you always think it will do more when you shoot your enemies and you always regret it when you shoot your friends.
—I didn't know we were rattling off aphorisms now. I thought the whole point of this garbage was to hash things out, not to disregard each other with useless sayings.
—I'm making a point about the violence inherently tied to cinematic images and the way they distort human relationships. I'm not the issue here. The issue is your disregard for anything that isn't immediately clarified.
—An aphorism is an aphorism is an aphorism is an aphorism.
—And an argument is an argument. Your point doesn't exist. All you're doing is dismissing anything that isn't your own idea.

Man, Oh Man looked at the projections above. They took a long drag from one another's cigarettes as the screen morphed into endless fever dreams. Organismal collages, purged mechanical forms, architecture made from bodies sewn together.

—If a camera is a gun, then the director must be a mob boss, and the cinematographer is a hit man.
—There's no need to turn the metaphor into an allegory.
—How many symbols do I need before it becomes an allegory?
—Three?
—Where did three come from? Is it another symbol? The rule of threes? If three is a symbol then you have four in total, and by then you're definitely an allegory.
—How is this then: the cinema camera is a gun.

—Is that all?

—On the surface, yes. Under that is a whole slew of things to talk about. Maybe they don't have to be metaphors on their own, but they oughta be talked about. How about the first bit is a metaphor and the rest is an explanation of what that metaphor means. No bits of aphorism attached.

—It's a good change to make. I don't know how real the argument is though.

—What does it matter if the argument is real? It just matters that the argument happens, that's all. Whether or not the cinema camera is a real gun means fuck-all to me.

—If it's a metaphor then it can't really be what you say it is.

—Yeah, yeah, yeah.

Man, Oh Man coughed into their sleeves, propped themselves off the wall, and walked away as the projections continued to screech behind them. They wandered the unreal city with their stride glued to the sidewalk, avoiding eye contact with the asphalt that bubbled in the street. Blocks of text rose to the surface.

—What if I avoid any type of eloquence and I just dictate my thoughts as is?

—Like what?

—End credits are the cause of cinema's systemic oppression of the viewing public.

—The form is better, but the statement itself is absurdist.

—Imagine trying to rise up against your oppressors when every piece of art you see ends with large blocks of white text overshadowing a mass of blackness. No matter how beautiful the film you just watched was, it's hard not to feel powerless when that same image of oppressive blocks appears.

—I can't figure out where you're even basing this argument. Who are the oppressors? Why are the blocks oppressive? What does the color matter? How else are they supposed to look?

—The oppressors are the bourgeoisie; the blocks are meant to mock the proletariat audience; the colors are a means of prioritizing the small percentage of wealth over the mass of the poor; I think the credits should not exist at all.

—Tell me that cinema is a gun again and I'll bite you. It'll annoy me, but I'll do it. Tell me that end credits are a tool for oppression and I'll spit the damned thing back out in your face.

—Is that a metaphor?

—Shut up. The point here is that you're garbage. The argument you're making reeks of conspiracy theorists and there's nothing real to back it up.

—We've been over this. It doesn't matter whether the argument is real. All that matters is that the argument can be made. It's absurd, but it can be made.

—What's the point then?

—The point is to make a point without any reason to do so.

II.

Man, Oh Man sat down on the edge of the sidewalk, looking out at the blocks of text that floated along the street surface, pulled by the asphalt currents. They moved from left to right. Left to right. Left to right. Always inching by too quickly to read, but just slow enough to catch a glimpse of three or so words. The two dipped their feet in and pieced the bits together as they passed.

—Marcel Duchamp invented the novel; his *Fountain* is the greatest novel I've ever seen.

—The closest that man ever got to a book was the time he drew a moustache on someone else's postcard of the Mona Lisa.

—If a good novel is just a good story, and a good story is one that adheres well to the conventions of storytelling, then a good novel is one that resembles a ready-made.

—You act as if there's no variety between Dickens and Homer.

—More than that. There isn't a single difference between Duchamp's *Fountain* and Dickens' novels. They're both just variations on manufactured products the artists were given. Maybe Dickens' took a little more time, but nonetheless it's the same idea.

—What do you want then?

—I don't know. Something new, I suppose.

—Is that what you think we are?

—I'm not here to push some holier-than-thou position. To be completely honest, we're just a dialogue. At our very best, we're some aimless and useless manifesto. What I'm saying is I'd like to see something the least bit new. Next time I read a novel, I don't want to feel sleepy by page twenty.

—You think plotless meandering will make you feel less sleepy?

—I think it's a good start.

One of the text blocks drifted onto the sidewalk, where Man, Oh Man kicked it back off into the street, watching it catch the current once more and flow out of sight. Another cigarette drag, another stub flicked onto the asphalt.

—A good start or not, it's still irresponsible to disregard a novelist just because they decided to write a story instead of a collage or something of the like.

—I think it works the other way around. If you're an adept writer, then it seems your duty to make something new.

—The point of literature isn't to see who can come up with the most original thing; the point of literature is to explore language and the complexities of humanity.

—I don't know about that. The whole thing seems overdone.

—The complexities of humanity seem overdone to you?

—They do.

—I think your brain fell into a river.

—If it did, then I might be better off. I'm tired of thinking about these things. It's a lose-lose situation. If I agree with you, then I fall back into a slump; if I disagree with you, then I'm acting out pretentiously. Without a mind, I get to just meander here for a bit and act out whatever ignorance I have.

III.

Man, Oh Man flickered in and out of existence, finding themselves stuck between the unreal city and crackling images of television static. Sidewalk panels went from concrete to white lines, then back. The conversationalists appeared, or acted, unimpressed.

They continued the pattern: stub, light, another drag, discarding the used butts in the current.

—When does it stop being a performance piece?
—It doesn't. It is one and it always has been and it always will be.
—That's garbage.
—Here: a world-renowned artist, hitting fifty or sixty, tells the world that he will be doing a new performance piece. He's going to own and operate a local hardware shop for three years. It'll be open to the public in a peripheral neighborhood in some small town, maybe one on the outskirts of a bigger city. He'll do it for a couple years, then he'll stop.
—Where's the art in that?
—It's art because he says it's art. What separates a Rothko from me painting my bedroom a couple of different shades of blue?
—That's a shit example and you know it is.
—I don't care whether the example is good or not. The point is that whether or not it's art doesn't matter. All art is ambiguously not art in my book. All good art is.
—Are you trying to police it now?
—I'm not. I'm just trying to say that anything counts as long as you put a name card next to it.

Man, Oh Man lit fresh cigarettes for one another, throwing the used matches behind their backs and taking in long drags. Again, the environment around them faded between form and sketch, occasionally reducing to black lines or materializing into concrete. Malfunctions took the form of rising trees as they flickered in and out.

—Is it still a performance if he does it for four years?
—It doesn't matter how long he does it for.
—What if he does one where he sits at home and files his taxes? Does it still count or does it only count if there's an audience to watch him do it?
—There's not always an audience in the hardware store. He has to save the money to lease a space, he has to sweep the floors after he closes the shop, open up in the morning.

—Yeah, but what if he never has an audience?

—He can be his own audience.

—It all feels so pseudo-intellectual. That whole spiel about "what is art?" that everyone tries to impress their mother with.

—I'm not trying to impress you, I'm trying to upset you.

A Set Of Obscured Images

I.

Man and Oh Man sat opposite one another, now chained to their setting of the café. Outside the room was nothing; inside the room was nothing. The two sat opposite of each other: floating oblivions. The surface between them twitched quietly. On top of it, an unplugged rotary phone. Man, Oh Man ignored each other bitterly; the phone rang. They pulled the earpiece up to one of their heads.

—Yes… I don't think either of us are up for it today… I'm sorry, I meant to say we're not up for it now… I guess whether or not it's today doesn't particularly matter… Fine, fine… Yeah…

Man, Oh Man set the phone down, crossed their legs, and faced each other, lighting their cigarettes separately, taking their drags in sync.

—If a place is more than one place, then what do I call it?
—Then you call it two places.
—But what if I want two places to be one place?
—Why would two be one?
—What if I live in a small one-bedroom apartment. One room is the bathroom, the next is the bedroom, and the last is the living room-kitchen area.
—Then you live in a three-room apartment.
—But is the last room a kitchen or a living room? Is it both? Or is there an invisible line that separates the living room part from the kitchen part?
—They're two separate rooms. You don't cook in the living room and you don't lounge in the kitchen.
—That's trash.

Man, Oh Man took a collective deep breath. The phone buzzed; cord swinging, dial rotating. At intervals, one would reach down to catch the cord while the other would jab their finger into the dial, trying to cease the movement. Each attempt deteriorated into frantic assaults, intercut with exhaustive grunts and moans. Man, Oh Man leaned back in their seats, starting fresh cigarettes.

—If a room is more than one, then it might as well be more than two. It's a living room and a kitchen and a dining room and a den and a sitting room and an art gallery.
—I don't know if I'd be willing to commit myself to anything more than two.
—Then there was no point in asking the question at all.

II.

—How can I tell whether or not someone's trash?
—Everyone is trash. The only way to be any better than that is to acknowledge it.
—Are we trash then?
—You are.

III.

Man, Oh Man sat across from each other, separated by chromatic walls that phased in and out of the visible spectrum. Flashes of the mirror image would appear; the two would look at one another, but not for long. One pushed the rotary off the tabletop, the other stomped out the noises.

—None of the Dadaists bothered following through as parents. I think we're all suffering from the consequences of it now.
—I don't know if it was their job to guide us any which way.
—Yeah, yeah, yeah. If you start something, if you fix something, then you ought to make sure that it keeps on going, make sure that it stays fixed. If the plumber says he'll fix the sink, you'd like it to stay fixed. Anyone can jury-rig a fucking sink.
—Was that one of the readymades?
—Yes. The sink is a readymade; Andre Breton used to be a plumber; Antonin Artaud fixed Bram Stoker's pipes; kicked out his voice box.

—Everything out of your mouth is vitriol.

—If a baby cries, then its mother and dada should be at the ready to tend to that baby. Your parents shouldn't just be around to fuck and then shoot you out. They better be ready to raise you too.

—We've found the right metaphor now? I'm glad we could.

—When Duchamp pulled *Fountain* out of the gutter and created the first novel, he should have been ready to raise that novel like it was his own. Instead, he just moved on and did his own thing, made his own work. He should've been nurturing the rest of us, keeping the damned thing alive.

—Yeah, yeah, yeah.

Man, Oh Man glanced up, looking to the center of the table, apathetically watching as old forms changed into new collages, shaped by vague figures. One stubbed his cigarette, the other lit a new one, ignited by the ashes of his previous.

—Do you recognize any of them?

—I recognize all of them; I don't necessarily like any of them, but I know all of them.

—What's the point of talking about any of this if you're going to hate everyone involved?

—It doesn't matter whether or not I like it. Things are what things are. They don't change depending on whether I like them or not.

—You're admirable.

—Fuck you too. I say things the way I do and that's that. Dada had a responsibility or it didn't. Who's to say? Who's not to say? Everything is duality. Paradox and doxa. It's all the same.

—You're speaking with your head against the table.

—Here is the way things work: we introduce ourselves (Man, Oh Man), the laugh track ensues, we talk with one another, say something witty or intellectual about art and shit, then we smoke a cigarette, change topic, and it repeats. That's it.

—What does it matter how things work? Structure is a foundation. You begin there and then put something together on top of it. Narrative is the same story told in different ways over and over again, yet it still holds up.

—I'm bored of narrative as well.

—Then you're the exception here.

—We both are. The two atemporal voices, sitting nowhere in particular, talking about nothing of any importance.

—When does it end?

—It doesn't. We repeat as a set of textile patterns. We will always be no one in particular, sitting nowhere in particular, talking about nothing of any importance. It's not about when things will end, it's about what we are to do next.

Man, Oh Man leaned back in their seats. The phone rang in spurts of ever-changing volume, moving from high to low and back again. While the two men continued smoking, one would nudge the rotary box, the other would try to ignore it. Fading images of light and face continued to flicker, albeit quieter now.

—Are we ever going to pick up the phone?

—It's not our place to decide whether we do or don't.

—Everything comes in twos nowadays, I guess, us included.

—If we pick up the phone, we aren't picking up the phone on our own accord, we're just continuing to follow whatever instructions were given to us. Things aren't so dynamic.

—Yeah, yeah, yeah.

IV.

Man, Oh Man disregarded eye contact. One fiddled with his fingernails, the other tapped his knuckles in morse code against the table, avoiding the rusted lyre lazily thrown over the phone as if it was a tarp or a curtain. They picked it up; fiddled with the strings lightly.

—If Orpheus is alone now, playing the lyre and all that garbage, does it matter that Eurydice existed in the first place?

—How do you determine whether something matters or not?

—I'm asking you.

—Working your way around a question doesn't mean you're asking the question yourself.

—I'm sure.

—There are three of Orpheus. There is one who never met Eurydice at all, there is one that is fucking Eurydice as we speak, and there's a third one where Eurydice was always lost to him. None of them know of the others. They all think they're the same person.

—If an Orpheus is more than one Orpheus, then what do you call him?

—The same thing you'd call him otherwise.

—Three lyres don't answer the question when they weren't mentioned in the first place.

—Eurydice only matters to the second Orpheus. The first one never met her and the third one's only heard of her. If she was never there, then she can't matter. If she is, then she can.

—How many of us are there?

—Maybe infinite, maybe one. Who's to say?

Man, Oh Man played with the lyre strings, plucking, then cutting them one by one, causing them to fray off into repellant curls. The room materialized and dematerialized around them as they leaned back in their chairs, wobbling back and forth in the spotlight, finding themselves occasionally on the edge, but then quickly pulled back.

—If there are three of Orpheus, how many are there of Daedalus?

—Of which Daedalus?

—How many are there?

—There are four and each of them are three?

—What separates the four from the other twelve smaller ones?

—One Daedalus built the labyrinth, another flew Icarus, another killed Minos, and the other tutored that Partridge kid, I think.

—I thought the fourth was the one that fucked Joseph Campbell to get over his son's death.

—I never know if I should call you an idiot or a sadist.

—If we knew what the two of them were like in bed together, I think we could get more specific. There's one Daedalus who never met Campbell, one who fucked him, and one who used to fuck him. The pattern isn't hard to catch onto.

—The point isn't to make it difficult to understand, the point is to make it true.

—Things are or aren't true. You can't force something into reality and make it so. We aren't god or anything like that. There are rules to everything.

—The rule is that I can make any claim I like and some part of it will be true. If the rest is false, I'll round up and it will all be fact.

—You're a sadist.

—I don't know whether I should bow or curtsy.

Man, Oh Man scratched away the table surface, wood chips piling around the base of the rotary phone, cord still swinging as a pendulum, unplugged. The walls faded in and out of view, flickering shades of blue and green, returning on occasion to certainty, then retreating to a blur.

—A picture of a cock is the same as a real cock.

—Is this made of the same rounding logic?

—The image is a representation of the reality. When the representation is brilliant, it becomes the real thing. Think about that Jeanne Dielman woman, the one who filmed herself doing housework for three or so days. It was reality.

—Jeanne Dielman isn't a real person. You're rounding up again.

—Whether or not she was doesn't matter. I was fooled by the art, so the art gets to be real now.

—That's the reward for good art?

—Maybe it is.

—Where does that put us?

—You're the picture of a cock and I'm the real thing.

V.

Man, Oh Man picked up the phone.

—What do you want?... Yes... Yes, we're through... Well, it doesn't matter whether or not you'd like things to go on, they won't... Yeah... The point is that we have nothing else to say right now... I know... He doesn't either... Yeah, yeah, yeah... I'll say it and then we're done… A pattern is a pattern, we're done for now, the loophole is there.

Man, Oh Man put the phone down, leaned back, and crossed their legs. The cord coiled around the base and the dial held itself tightly in place; another call came in, but neither bothered to answer.

—If there was ever a manifesto worth shit, I haven't seen it yet.

The phone continued to ring.

People Man, Oh Man Would Rather Talk To

—No one at all.
—Someone calm and slow.
—A prophet in the midst of his prophetic fever dream.
—Someone they never really knew all that well.
—The Belvedere Torso.
—A pantheon of lesser gods.
—Norman Mailer after he's already died.
—The voice from the radio.
—Cassandra.
—A man with a bowl of fish for a head.
—Anybody else.

Exhaustion

I.

Man, Oh Man leaned back, exhausted, not thinking about anything at all, desperately trying not to speak. They rubbed their eyes and coughed into their elbows.

—I'm sick of things not happening, these un-happenings.
—They're non-happenings.
—I hate you to the core of the planet and back. My limbs are sore, wherever they are.
—If it was an un-happening, then the event would be in some weird spot of neither happening nor not happening. It'd be some idiotic version of Schrodinger's Cat. If it's non-happening, then the situation is clear and concise.
—Nothing I've thought of so far has been clear and concise; it's been un-clear.
—It's been non-clear. The thoughts have been blurry, not half and half.
—At this point, it feels like you're trying to flaunt some non-existent intellectual muscle, but it's just clumsily flopping around instead.
—Are you saying I need to work out more?
—I'm saying that you're an idiot. And worse than that, you're just forming a bunch of un-starters.
—Non-starters.
—Un-starters. They seem to be going somewhere but they aren't, they're just hints shooting off in various directions, pretending to be meaningful. You're the definition of pretentious.
—If I am, then you are.
—I am.

Man, Oh Man wiped their eyes and looked at each other, ignoring the smokiness of the room and the increasing ambiguity of this space.

II.

—I'm all turned around now.
—Stop meandering.

III.

Samuel Beckett laid along the tabletop, between the two chainsmokers, blinking and wheezing. Man, Oh Man tapped their knuckles against the wood and their feet against the tile.

—Have you ever considered a narrator who isn't floating around in oblivion?

Samuel Beckett said nothing.

—I think I'd be more interested if you made the poor bastard trip over his shoelace and fall down some bottomless pit instead.
—What's the difference between that and oblivion?
—Well, now he'd be falling. The sensation would make things more physically terrifying.
—Yeah, but if something is physically terrifying for too long, then it's just existentially terrifying again.
—Yeah, yeah, yeah.

Samuel Beckett rolled onto his stomach, lifted his chest, and pulled his knees under. He sat in the center of the table. Man, Oh Man looked at one another.

—This isn't getting anywhere?
—When did that become obvious to you?

Hearsay

I.

Man, Oh Man sat across from one another, one holding a glass jar in his hand, whispering into it, putting his hand over the top and then pulling it up to his ear to listen. The other cracked his knuckles and sipped his coffee, occasionally looking back at the empty counter.

—I don't know where we're supposed to go from here, what we're supposed to talk about, speculate about, avoid. I feel completely lost.
—You don't feel lost, you feel unfound.
—I already hate you enough as you are, you don't have to turn into some kind of Orwellian puppet.
—As if there's some kind of shadowy government lurking over me? I don't even know if we can cast shadows, let alone act on behalf of them.
—It doesn't have to be a government in order for it to be double speak. You're changing words to fit your agenda, the authorial agenda, whatever.
—I like to think that I'm not acting on his behalf.
—There are no choices in a book, no matter what you say or I say. The end of the book is still the end of the book. More than reality, our circumstances are set in stone. You don't get to decide.
—Are you a fatalist now?
—No, I just know how to follow things to their logical conclusion.
—You must've passed the third grade with flying colors. Did they give you a star? A medal? You deserved one.
—I didn't pass the third grade, I unfailed it.
—You're a complete bastard, and I think you ought to know.
—Maybe I'd be a better person if you didn't try to push some type of bullshit agenda every time we spoke to one another. I hate it.
—Whatever happened to it being out of my control? I thought the author was doing all this. How can you blame me for anything I ever do?

—At this point, I don't care; I'd rather talk about why you feel it's necessary to push a new set of words on me. Thinking about my own existence makes me nauseous.

—I hope you stay that way: unwell, unhappy, unhealthy. I don't think they're new words. Putting 'un' in front of something doesn't change the whole lexicon or anything like that.

—No, they don't, but they change the mood of it. 'Unwell' is less negative than 'sick' is; they have different feelings tied to them. When I think of 'unwell' I just think that the person is anything but well, and that they'll be well again. When I think of 'sick' I imagine someone hunched over the toilet vomiting.

—I didn't know you'd taken it upon yourself to personalize every word you know.

—I think everybody has.

—I know I haven't.

Man, Oh Man continued performing their tasks: one listening to the glass jar, occasionally hitting it against the tabletop when it wasn't working, the other twiddling his thumbs, rolling his eyes, tapping his foot, doing whatever to pass the time.

—If you're going to go out of your way to make up these words, or exchange them for other words, then you might as well change the language entirely.

—The action is a bit more nuanced than that. They're not new words, just different combinations.

—You're just a hodge-podge of portmanteaus; it seems lazy.

—I don't care how much work goes into it; trying to turn it into its own language would just feel like some even stupider version of pig latin.

—It seems like the thing to do.

—The function isn't to be eccentric, just to convey the point better.

—I imagine you speaking as some babbling algorithm stuck on 'un' words, trying to connect all of them, yet unable to. You might not be smart enough to convey a point.

—Are clear and smart the same thing? I'd be intimidated by the glass if that were the case; thankfully there's none around here.

—How would it go?
—The Orwell language?
—Yeah.
—If it had to exist, to have some type of consistent form, then I think it would slowly rotate between the words like a pocket watch, or a limp arm. It'd cling to a surface, stay for a moment, and then swing again and cling to the next surface. Here:

> Unwed are unhappy, unhappy are unwed, unwed are unwed, the unhappy are unhappy, the unhappy unwed, and unwed undone, undone unhappy, the unwed are undone, undone are unhappy, unhappy are unwed, unwed, unhappy, unhappy are undone, the undone undone unhappy, yet the unhappy are unpleased, the unpleased are unhappy and unwed, the unwed are undone, and the undone are unpleased and unhappy, they are unwed and undone, unpleased by the unwed and the unhappy and undone by the ungood, ungood are unpleased, unhappy are ungood, unwed are unpleased are ungood, the unwed are ungood, unpleased are unhappy, unhappy are ungood, ungood are ungood, unwed are unpleased and undone, ungood are undone, unwed are unhappy, ungood are unwed, undone are unhappy, unpleased are unwed, ungood are undone, unhappy are unhappy, unhappy, unwed, unpleased, all unpleased, unhappy, the undone are unpleased and unwed, they are ungood, ungood and undone, unhappy and unpleased, unpleased, yes, unpleased, unwed and unhappy, the unhappy are unwed, unwed are unhappy, ungood, undone, unpleased, ungood are unwed, unwed are unhinged, unhinged are unpleased, unhinged are ungood, undone, unpleased, unhappy, the unhinged, unhinged and unhappy and undone and unwed and unpleased, the unpleased and unwed and undone and unhappy

40

are unhinged, ungood are undone, unhappy are
unwed, unwed are unhappy, unhinged are
unhappy, unpleased are unhinged, unhinged are
unwed, are unpleased, are unhappy, are unhinged,
that and undone.

—I hate how aphoristic you tend to be. You're pulling language
out of your ass. Stuffing yourself into otherwise empty spaces.
—The aphorisms are there, they had to be, but maybe they've been
undercut at the same time. Does it still count as an aphorism if I
don't believe it? When it's disingenuous?
—It's utterly aggravating. None of this did anything, it's just static
on a television, you just had to fill your mouth with something and
decided on this bland pudding.

Man, Oh Man set down the glass jar, and put away their time
wasters. Mise-en-scène returned to its default. They sat across from
one another, did nothing, faded in and out of reality, briefly fell
into abstraction, then returned and maintained the kind of
fluctuation which has defined their place in this café.

—I'm sick of any language, whether you've made it up or not. I'd
just like to leave.
—You're always so quick to get fed up with things. You never just
absorb the circumstance and move forward. You're always inclined
to hold onto it for a bit too long.
—It seems like the right thing to do.
—Oh, shut up.
—I wish I could, but instead I have to talk to you.
—What's the point of talking to each other for so long? Other than
for the sake of the author? I don't know what else there is to talk
about, or if there's anything meaningful to say.
—You could ask me whether or not I think you're complete trash.
—Do you think I'm complete trash?
—It's the only thing I think about. Every other thought turns my
brain to mush, except that one.
—Yeah, yeah, yeah.

—The whole thing, the whole book, just feels like some kind of sadistic playground. He's prodding us with all of the ideas he comes up with when he's stoned or drunk, and then he expects us to enjoy the puppetry of it all.

—On the bright side, maybe they'll be something that outdoes us, that he decides he'd rather use instead. I hope it's good enough that he never bothers revisiting.

—There's always someone to come back and visit, maybe not the author, but there's always someone.

—You're proverbial, you're generalized, you're aphoristic.

—I like the way we were speaking before, whichever one of us said it, the part where we just rambled to ourselves in double speak. I think it was the best thing that's come about so far, we didn't have to think about anything or pretend to talk.

—It's as if you want me to feel sympathy, even knowing that there's no way I ever could.

> Unwed are unhappy, unhinged are unhappy, unpleased are unhinged, unhinged are unwed, are unpleased, are unhappy, are unhinged, unpleased are unwed, unwed are unpleased, unhinged are unhappy, unhappy are unpleased, unwed are undone, undone are unpleased, undone are unhinged, unhinged are undone, are unhappy, are unsatisfied, undone are unsatisfied, unsatisfied are undone, unwed are unsatisfied, unpleased are unsatisfied, unsatisfied are unpleased, are undone, are unhinged, the unhinged unsatisfied, unpleased, undone, unhappy, undone are unhinged, unhinged are unsatisfied, unpleased are unsatisfied, and the unsatisfied are unpleased, and unhappy, and undone, and unwed, the unwed are unsatisfied, the unsatisfied are unwed, the undone undone, unhinged unhinged, unsatisfied are undone, unhinged.

—I'm not sure if you're a real person or just some assemblage of the language games I used to play when I was a little kid.
—I don't know how else you expect me to present myself, if not through the things I say.
—I don't want you to present yourself at all.

II.

Man, Oh Man reflected briefly, lapsing in upon themselves, mentally twisting like a mobius strip that traces its way from point 'a' to point 'b', weeding through all of the hysterical thoughts that have come out of their mouths.

—There's a bull in a china shop. He owns the place with his mother, it was passed down to him by his father.
—No. In a china shop, there is a bull.
—The second half was fine?
—The shop was passed down to him by his father, he now owns it with his mother.
—What if I want it to be arranged in the opposite way? His mother should be mentioned first and then his father.
—Why bother putting them in any particular order?
—If we say the bit about the father first, then he's receiving a hand-me-down life. If we say the bit about the mother first, then he's participating in the family business.
—What's the difference? One or the other, he's still miserable.
—If he's unhappy, it should be arranged from bad to worst. You want the circumstances to come across as a downward spiral.
—So he inherited the shop from his father and works it with his mother. They don't like one another, but when the father died she came with her son to the funeral.
—Is the work worse than the inheritance?
—He works the shop with his mother, inherited it from his father. They don't like one another, but when the father died she came with her son to the funeral.
—It might be worse to live a mundane life than it is to go to a lone funeral.

—His mother will die too.

—Is she currently dead?

—I don't know. She could be.

—So he went to his father's funeral, and inherited the shop, which he worked in with his mother for years, before she, too, passed away.

—The mother's death is worse than the mundanity is worse than the father's death?

—No, but the order sounds better.

—The father died; the mother died; the bull worked at the shop, which he inherited from one, and used to work in with the other.

—I think that sounds better than anything we've said so far.

—Yeah, yeah, yeah.

Man, Oh Man leaned back in their seats, flicked their cigarettes across the table at one another, and sighed heavily. One rubbed his knuckles against the table until his skin wore away, the other gritted his teeth into dust.

—What's the point of the bull if he spends his whole life in a china shop?

—It's so you have something to be terrified of. The bull doesn't exist, just the sentences about him do.

—Do we exist?

—Who cares? What would it matter either way? 'Yay, we don't exist' or 'oh no, we do'?

—I think I'd want it to go vice versa.

—It's as if you see the purpose of the statement coming at you, and then, right before it hits, you duck out of the way.

—This existential shit isn't the point. The point is that there is a bull in a china shop, whose life ought to be arranged in the order of their depressive natures.

—We've already done this.

—What about his kids?

—I don't care.

—One is married in a different city, and the other two live nearby and work the shop.

—The order's correct enough.

—Here: The father died; the mother died; the bull worked at the shop which he inherited from one and used to work in with the other. Now his eldest son has moved away, while the other two have stayed behind to help run the business.
—What would a bull do with a china shop?
—I don't think it really matters. All I care about is that his life is miserably empty and uneventful.
—You're resentful toward metaphors.
—He's been around as long as we have and I don't like that.

III.

Man, Oh Man sat across from one another, as they always do, as they always will. Between them stood a trio of robed men, arms crossed behind their backs, chins raised, looking forward. Man, Oh Man ignored them, instead looking blankly into the distance and smoking their cigarettes.

—Man, Oh Man sat together, they talked, and then they stopped when they were done.
—Who the fuck are they?
—The Roman chorus tells you things how they ought to be.
—I agree that we ought to be out of here, but I don't need someone lurking behind me, reminding me about all of my problems.
—Maybe it's a good thing now. The only time I remember choruses showing up is when the bit is proclaimed a tragedy.
—You'd like to be a tragedy?
—No, but it's good to be recognized as one finally; there's nothing pleasant about any of this.
—Man, Oh Man walked to the door and exited the café. When they got outside, the sun was very bright; they shielded their eyes with their hands.
—If they say things how they ought to be, then we might not even be a tragedy. Maybe we just ought to be a tragedy.
—We're a tragedy.
—Or we ought to be.

—The sounds that come out of your mouth are so guttural and distracting. It's hard to concentrate.

—Concentrate on what? The conversation? The chorus?

—Either? Both? Whichever one has nothing to do with you talking.

—Man, Oh Man walked down the sidewalk together until they reached the corner, where they shook hands, smiled, and parted ways.

—The perfect place for these three would be in a stage play, standing behind all of the action with their microphones muted.

—What would the play be?

—I don't think it particularly matters.

—Why would they be muted?

—The play would be about two men standing in the middle of the stage, talking about how they don't know where they are. There'd be a dead body on the floor, they'd accuse one another of the murder. Blah blah blah. Then every time the lights turned black, another body, or a couple more, would appear on the stage.

—The chorus would be alive?

—And it would go on and on until there were so many bodies on the stage that they could barely move around, the actors would become upset, the real actors, they'd cuss and they'd try to storm off the stage, but they wouldn't be able to because of all the bodies in the way.

—The chorus would be alive?

—They'd sit in the background somewhere and list off all of the possible ways that the bodies got there.

—Man, Oh Man met up the next day at the café and continued to talk with one another, happily sharing stories from their youth, drinking coffee, smoking cigarettes.

—Their tone always sounds so patronizing. I hate it.

—I'd rather fantasize about the stage play than listen to them speak in real life, or about it.

Man, Oh Man closed their eyes, continuing to smoke, butting their heads against the table, crushing the cigarettes between their teeth and the wood grain. They stopped and rubbed their temples while the Roman chorus remained in place, ignoring any kind of emotional display.

—Are they saying that we ought to be happy or that we ought to be just like regular old people?
—The point is that we are regular old people.
—That's idiotic. We've been sitting here forever and haven't even taken the time to eat. All we've done is smoke and talk about nothing.
—I don't want to do either.
—Where is the realism then? Is it just speculative bullshit now?
—You're a melodramatic pile of trash. We're metaphors for human interaction.
—Oh yeah? Is the metaphor that everyone is just sitting and talking? Not doing anything? That's garbage. Is it that the real hell is mundanity? Nope. Is it that mundanity is humanity? Fuck that.
—Man, Oh Man finished their conversation, split the bill, and parted ways, not seeing one another again until the following week.
—I hate you.
—The Roman chorus thinks we ought to be doing something more.
—Then why do we still come and talk to each other at the café?
—Because of some residual masochism.
—Is this masochism?
—It's masochism because I keep replying to you and continuing the conversation.
—Man, Oh Man moved away from one another, lived out their lives, and then died far away, surrounded by their loving families.
—We ought to be dead.
—I can only fantasize about some level of reality where we never existed in the first place. It's the only pleasant thing I can think of.

IV.

—The father died; the mother died; the bull worked at the shop which he inherited from one and used to work in with the other.

Now his eldest son has moved away, while the other two have stayed behind to help run the business.

—His kids have kids and they help run the shop, none of them ever become notable or even particularly happy, they instead just run the china shop, pass it down from one generation to the next, until the family tree shrivels up and dies.

.

Intentions

I.

Man, Oh Man coughed into their sleeves, glanced up at one another, then dug into their pockets. One found cigarettes, the other found a pocket book, which was filled with short aphorisms from various accomplished writers and thinkers. He paged through it, sighing after each sentiment he read.

—I think if we read all this backwards, the whole universe would tear itself apart.
—One can only hope.
—I'm tempted to, but the thought of performing the gesture, most gestures, feels obscene.
—Is writing backwards a gesture or an action?
—A gesture is the thought of the action, the action is itself. Just don't think about it.
—I already am.
—Then you're obscene. Looking at you is nauseating. I couldn't figure it out before, I assumed it was your face, but now I get it: your sheer existence is pornographic and indulgent.
—Is it still a gesture if the action never happens? If I never go through with it?
—I think so. Otherwise, all gestures would just be passing thoughts, before you go to bed.
—So it can't be the thought of the action. If it was, then I'd just be the thoughts you have before sleeping. I think I'm more than that. I'm not sure, but I think I am.
—You're nothing but a bum, chain-smoking in a café somewhere. There's nothing particularly interesting about you.
—You're a dull bastard.
—If you turned those aphorisms around, reflected them in a mirror, they'd end up describing the disgusting way you slouch in your chair. If they did anything else, I'd blame the image for being bent or obscured.
—Does that turn me into the gesture?

—I'm not sure that I care what you are. I'm so goddamn exhausted already. I don't know how much longer we can go on. We're as outdated as VHS players, or novellas.

Man, Oh Man tore out the aphorisms one by one, shredding the pages into thin strips and cramming them into fortune cookies, *aphorism is the universal truth condensed into language*. One sipped his coffee while the other threw up onto the tile floor.

—Backwards they just turn into gibberish: language into condensed truth universal the is aphorism. Is that even an aphorism? Just a declarative statement?
—Right now it's nothing, and I think it's better that way.
—Maybe not backwards, just rearranged in the proper way: language into condensed truth, universal is the aphorism.
—You've barely changed the previous one, just added a comma, flipped two words around.
—That was the intention.
—Now it's just returned to aphorism. You've made a big circle back to the trash we started with.
—Things still need to feel universal.
—Says who? The aphorism? Why not make it do a handstand and watch its head explode with paint?
—I don't remember that. Did that already happen?
—It would have had to.
—If there's enough paint, you could flood the entire universe.
—Would that change anything?
—It might. Who could say? I've never destroyed the universe before, I've only sat in the waiting room with those loud clocks.
—Are you the poet now?
—The colloquial one or the one that's currently acting out?
—Either.
—Paranoia tells me that I'm both, and that you're just the carcass of the former. I don't know where else these painful little proverbs would come from.
—Yeah, yeah, yeah.

Man, Oh Man snatched one of the book pages and blew their nose with it, wiping the coarse paper against their nostrils, then crumpling it up and throwing it across the room, back into the dark corners where one could only assume that the walls were connecting. They pulled cigarettes out of their pockets and took a drag.

—If you want things to become universal, be the colloquial poet, make everything specific and intimate.
—I think that's against the point here.
—If you do it enough times, then it can't help but be universal. If the subjects and topics are infinite, then everyone is bound to latch onto something.
—It seems so disingenuous.
—So does universality. Are you the hive mind? Can you relate to everyone? Have you done everything?
—Enough, I think.
—The theory that we're god, that the two of us are, feels as if it's on the edge of being true. We have the collective cynicism it calls for. The only thing to refute it is your constant idiocy.
—Who says that stupid isn't the universal? We could all be idiots.
—I think you're trash.
—Are those the same thing?
—One is acceptable, inevitable. The other is your own choice. It's the product of your oversentimental declarations.

II.

Man, Oh Man took turns glancing past the kino eye, hoping to catch it in their peripheries. Spiteful toward their circumstances, the conversationalists did not want to confront the viewer directly. Each took a drag and wiped the ashes off their laps.

—What's the point here? They were already aware of us.
—But now they are moreso.
—Are they? We haven't left them out of the conversation. They've been here with us the whole time, knowingly.

—The fourth wall is shattered, not directly, something we said ricocheted and cracked it. Now they can see us through one of the peepholes.

—I think poetry is meant to be read on the side when you feel melancholy, not when your desire is to explain circumstance. The fourth wall is garbage.

—So are you.

—It'd be better for everyone if it wasn't there in the first place. Better yet, put it behind them, next to the entryway. Let everyone sit on stage. I can't stand this game of pretend where we ignore everyone watching us.

—It's not a game, it's etiquette.

—All you're doing is turning the lot of them into a pack of voyeuristic perverts "looking through the peephole." You act as if the act of reading and watching is disgusting.

—Peepholes are intimate.

Man, Oh Man closed one eye and looked across the table at one another; the cigarette smoke steeped upwards and made them squint; their chairs creaked at any hint of movement. The wood would rub against itself and the two would squirm, only causing more sound, trapping them in an endless cycle of action and reaction.

—If the fourth wall is behind the audience, someone could still be peeking in from the lobby.

—The lobby doesn't exist; the theater doesn't exist; the goddamn planet doesn't. The point here is the concept: fourth walls are trash. The first, second, third, they're all trash.

—It's there whether you like it or not.

—Yeah, yeah, yeah.

—It's a good thing too.

—I'd rather the thing happen in the middle of a field somewhere. It'd feel more honest that way. At this point I feel like a buffoon bullshitting the carnival crowd.

—You might as well be; it would fit you better than the complaining does.

—Complaining is the only way things get done. If you're upset, then why not bring it to light? Otherwise no one will bother fixing the problem.

—What if there isn't a problem in the first place?

—There's always a problem: the water is too cold; I burned the roof of my mouth; someone locked me out of the apartment building; I was late to a meeting.

—What if the problem doesn't matter then?

Man, Oh Man spit their coffee out onto the floor, took another sip, and spit again, repeating themselves as if glitched or broken. They rubbed their eyes, looking up again past the kino eye.

—This is beside the point. What I was saying before is that the fourth wall is a bunch of nonsense. What I want isn't that big of a deal. It can't be. I want the audience to sit on stage with us, to participate.

—You're forcing them into a position they don't want to be in.

—You're forcing them to sit complacently on the sideline.

—The stage is directly in front of the audience.

—All I'm saying is that if they hate me, I'd rather they say it to my face than nudge the person next to them and whisper it. Shout it in my goddamn face. Chew me out.

III.

Man, Oh Man sifted through a table of cigarettes, filing through the filters as if secretaries for the day, looking at each fleck of tobacco, sorting which ones seemed to be decaying and which seemed to be fresh.

—All concept art is just an expression of bureaucracy.

—You always seem eager to make declarative statements; not to say that I see myself any differently, but still.

—Think about that one Paul Auster book, not the one he wrote, the one that someone highlighted over. They ran through and put a different color over each of the proper nouns, then took out the words. I don't remember which book they did it to.

—It sounds like a waste of time. Think of that image, where someone just sits at their computer overusing the highlighter tool.
—All art is a waste of time. We could be working instead. Regardless, the point here is that he must've just spent hours sifting through the words, finding which things to mark, what color to make them. It's like having to annotate a book without any good reason to.
—What was the statement he was trying to make?
—I don't know. But I think in the end it was probably worth it, as much as any art is. The thing was beautiful, I felt like I was leafing through a rainbow of emotions.
—Did you read it?
—I don't know how I'd go about doing that.
—You're so fashionable. Too fashionable. Always trying to mutate someone else's art into your own. They're not your words, stop repurposing them.
—You say it as if that wasn't the point of reading.

IV.

Man, Oh Man sat across from one another clicking their tongues, refusing to match each other's cadence, and aggravating the room as a result. The rest of the café was filled with the static remnants of previous patrons. Ghosts lingering in space.

—He's a giant statue made out of piss and shit.
—I don't like him either, but there's no need to insult him; you're just gonna cause the situation to degrade further.
—The author wants to write me out, so be it. Good luck figuring out who's who. I can't remember myself at this point.
—He could just kill the both of us.
—And spend the rest of the thing describing the setting, the empty room?
—He has the right to.
—Yeah, yeah, yeah. Once the novel is done, the author is unimportant. His opinion doesn't matter; his intentions don't matter. He no longer has a say in what any of it means.

—If he was born in New York City, raised by an Italian family, I'd like to know.
—Why? The man's somewhere else right now. He isn't concerned. We're on our own.
—What does it matter? He was here at some point. That's important to note. Are we important to the story when we leave? Doesn't it matter that we were a part of it?
—We aren't the producer, we're the product. There's a difference. The product is important to itself. The producer is only temporary.
—Were you talking or throwing up? Everything that's coming out of your mouth is made of muttled sounds. None of it means anything, as much as you want to pretend that it does.
—The man has no idea what he's doing. He pours trash onto the page and others misconstrue it as truth and depth.

Man, Oh Man tapped their knuckles against the table, impatiently looking around the room, waiting for something to happen, or something to change, some variation in their current endeavour. There has always been some level of fatigue, but never this much. Man, Oh Man are exhausted. Man, Oh Man aren't sure if they can even open their jaws anymore. So much has already come out and so little has happened because of it. They think about stopping, but compulsions prevent them. The conversation continues, knowing that it has nowhere else to go.

—Andy Warhol didn't know a damn thing about what he was doing.
—Was he the guy who wrote all of this trash? I thought he only ever did pop art.
—Someone else did, but the point I'm trying to make is that no artist ever understands the thing they're doing. They just futz around with something until someone compliments them on it.
—Yeah, yeah, yeah.
—The guy was an utter failure. He was the capitalist fucking dream boy. Poster boy.
—Everyone and their mother is the capitalist dream. Get over yourself.

—Him moreso. The guy made soup cans into art for fucksake. What's more consumerist than turning every ordinary product into a piece of art? He glorified consumerism, made it seem like everything you bought was special.

—Andy Warhol's a tragedy. He's the over-glorified factory worker who never did enough, always fell flat on his daily quota. He was the ever-distracted proletariat. The man's a sad metaphor.

—No, no, no. He's the sad symbol.

—What's the difference between a symbol and a metaphor?

—A symbol has a face, and a metaphor has an ass.

—I don't understand.

—Warhol's a symbol because he's a person you can picture in your head, he's a real thing that represents an idea. A metaphor is a hypothetical image that represents an idea. There isn't really a bull in a china shop.

—There is. His mother is dying of cancer and his father spends the day taking care of her. The bull was overwhelmed by the stress and gutted his own china shop.

—Your body is filled to the brim with bullshit.

The floor creaked. Man, Oh Man perked their ears and looked around; the room was still empty. They rubbed their eyes, looking tiredly at one another. One checked the clock and the other rubbed his temples. 13:13. The hands didn't move.

—If the author doesn't matter, then we might as well be made of the real ink on the actual paper.

—You say it like it isn't true.

—I hope it isn't. I try to act like it isn't.

—We're made in a document that's been reproduced who knows how many times. If everything goes our way, some of those documents are real. Things you could touch.

—I'd rather we didn't exist in the first place. It would be easier to be nothing, return to the ether and just wallow in the ground as substance.

—In order to do that, they have to print us, use us up, toss us off to the wayside. You can't decay without physicality. It's the law.

—Is it now? I thought the law was eternal damnation in a café?

—It's both. There will always be some iteration of us. It could be the print copy, it could be the digital copy. Pieces of us can disappear, but the originals, the two of us, will always be stuck here talking about nonsense, arguing, getting nowhere, and then taking a moment to breathe before starting over again.

—Books don't go on forever. Eventually they stop.

—Odysseus will never stop sailing home. When he gets there, the book restarts.

—I think that's trash. That you are. I am.

—Self-deprecation is the only genuine form of modesty.

Man, Oh Man took deep breaths, inhaling slowly, exhaling quickly. They fiddled with their cigarettes, unrolling them then repacking them, lighting the tobacco then blowing it out. The table shook annoyingly. Man, Oh Man responded, taking a drag and then flicking their cigarettes past one another.

—I feel kind of numb now.

—You're stealing the seat out from under the audience. Put it back.

—I haven't done anything other than react. You've spent the whole conversation talking out of your ass, pretending to be nihilistic, murmuring about idiotic things.

—There's no reason to talk unless it's coming out of your ass. If it's out of your mouth, then it's just puke, regurgitated food. If it comes out of your ass it means that you've digested it.

—So shit is the digested idea? I'm going to rip my hair out.

—Close your mouth. Try again.

—Now you're speaking in tongues. Everything coming out of your mouth—ass—is just eccentric gibberish. You're talking in some derivative language. It's not comprehensible, but bits and pieces are still present.

—Yeah, yeah, yeah.

—Is that the colloquial apathy now?

—I think so. You're not worth a thoughtful response so it just seems easier to dismiss the statement entirely. You aren't worth the breath.

—You flatter me.

V.

Man, Oh Man sat in the café, surrounded by unmarked gravestones, all arranged in geometrically perfected formations, straight from every angle. The walls around them dissolved into a dull gray. The two kept a lookout over one another's shoulders, squinting their eyes, trying to see through the smoke screen.

—Every graveyard is just a collage of human bodies, nature, and stones.
—It's rude to walk all over people's art, best not to visit your dead relatives then.
—You're taking my sentiment in the wrong direction.
—Of course I am.
—If you can walk over a collage, then you have a right to walk over whatever else you want to.
—If I don't visit graveyards?
—Then you might as well sit in the café and do nothing until you rot away.
—I will.

Man, Oh Man stood up and wiped the smoke and ashes from their clothes. They sat back down. One closed his eyes and fiddled in his head with the thought of leaving; the other absent-mindedly scratched the tabletop, looking around, ignoring the gravestones that still surrounded them.

—What someone ought to do is dig up that collage and take all the jaws off the skeletons.
—You're making my temples sore.
—Everybody's so worried about creating the right voice, whatever the shit they're making demands. I say if it's so important, they might as well go out to the graveyard and get some samples.
—You talk through your mandible?
—Everyone does; you are right now.
—I'm not talking at all.

—A smart writer would take each one of those jaws, clip it onto their own skull, and take it out for a spin. If you don't use outside sources then you're just talking out of your ass, making assumptions about what other people might sound like.

—What's the point of pronouncing the words if you're just going to be writing them down?

—Someone else might read them outloud. Someone else inevitably will.

—I'm bound to be dictated?

—Everyone and their mother is.

—I can only hope she isn't bound to dictate. I think it'd be best if they didn't dig up her grave, left her jaw attached and in the ground.

—Then how would we ever know what she sounded like?

Man, Oh Man leaned toward one another, across the table, blowing smoke in each other's faces, increasingly detached from their setting, the unmarked graves which had slowly begun to back away, retreating into the soft edges of the café.

—What happens if you put on two jaws at once?

—Then you'd turn out like King Charles, speaking in poems some Russian man gave you.

—You're turning into nonsense.

—Or you'd end up like Bill Shakeshisbeard, in love with words. He spent all of his time pronouncing each and every syllable until his flesh rotted away, and his jaw fell off. Someone caught the thing before it hit the ground and threw it on their own skull. Every bastard with a sonnet is just the next person to catch that rotting mouth.

—You're a broken moralist.

—I'm not moralizing, I'm just telling you how things tend to turn out.

VI.

—How should these things function?

—They should not.

Vaudeville

I.

—The way that you act is utterly stupid. The way that you just sit there and smoke, meander around topics, say whatever idiot thing comes to mind, I can't stand it.

—I'd rather you just don't say anything at all.

Man, Oh Man sat in their seats, now facing the wall, formally undefined, acting as a red curtain behind the vaudevillian displays: artists making a mockery of themselves, esoterically looking for some kind of meaning, Luis Buñuel walked out from the darkness, standing just in front of the void, on the edge of it. He looked at the two, bowed separately to each, to one, then the other. He adjusted his posture, making sure that it looked elegant and intentional.

Happy. Buñuel slowly smiled, raising the corners of his mouth upward, relaxing his eyelids, displaying the two central teeth that turned slightly inward toward one another. Ears perked, bits of hair scattered along the top of his head, skin wrinkling at the edges of his eyes; his top lip curled over the gums, forming a straight, soft line. He held his hand under his chin, palm opened, acting as a pedestal for this facial display. Happy. He looked at one man and then the other. Happy. Buñuel returned to a blank expression and bowed to each of the two individually.

Unhappy. The corners of his mouth dropped down, unattended, teeth covered by the lips, the bags under his eyes drooping down, puffing up as the nuanced display of tossing and turning, the events of the previous night, his eyebrows hung low, eyes sunken in, the pupils looking around aimlessly, chin now seemingly wider and flat bottomed, ear lobes hanging lazily. Buñuel inhaled slowly, rubbed his knuckles against his eyes, and exhaled, looking nowhere in particular. He rose his hand again as a pedestal below his chin. Unhappy. He took a step forward and turned his head to one man and then the other, then stepped back, waited a moment, and reverted to the blank expression. He bowed.

Man, Oh Man glanced at one another, trading cigarettes, lighting the ends, and taking a drag, inhaling, exhaling, inhaling, exhaling, tapping the butt against the ashtray. They continued to watch the performance, hinting occasionally at some kind of reaction.

Sad. He relaxed his jaw, letting it hang loosely, mouth slightly opened, flattening and stretching the space between his nose and his lip, the philtrum clearly defined, structurally prominent; his eyes returned to the previous state: sunken in, heavy bags beneath, puffed up and dragging his brow downward, the pupils wandering around the room, avoiding any particular meaning. Sad. Again: the hand under the chin, the step forward, the turn toward one viewer, then the other, the step back, and the return to the blank expression.

Melancholy. A new expression: relaxed mouth, closed lips, flat chin, unfocused eyes slowly lowering to the ground, face wrinkling, pale complexion, flat forehead. Melancholy. He displayed the expression to the two, and returned to the default face. He waved to the viewers, arm fully stretched, bowed again, over and over, then stood back up and returned to the blackened café wall.

II.

The next figure emerged from the void: Tom Waits meandering into view, chin to chest, looking at the ground, tired eyes. He wore black slacks, and a leather jacket over a white button up, snap-brim fedora holding down his unkempt hair. He looked around the room—ducking his head under the table, peeking behind the counter—then returned to the void. He emerged again moments later, dragging a chair behind him. He stopped at the table and sat, crossing his arms over the backrest, straddling the seat. He reached across the table and pulled the ashtray to the edge of the surface.

Man, Oh Man ignored him, passing the time by scratching the various parts of their face, rubbing their knuckles against their eyes, tapping the table, sighing, and so on. One lit a cigarette while the other played with the matchbox, filing his nails against the friction strip; he'd finish one, inspect it, and move onto the next, never making any noticeable progress.

Tom Waits exhaled and started patting around his jacket, checking the pockets, turning them inside out, until he found his own pack. He took out a cigarette and flicked it into his mouth, then snatched the matchbox and ignited the cigarette, closing his eyes and inhaling slowly. He ignored the two men on either side of him. He took another cigarette out, stuck it in his mouth, lit it. Another cigarette, another cigarette, another cigarette. A spotlight formed around him. The act:

> Inhale: drag; hold; exhale; release. Inhale, inhale: drag, drag; hold, hold; exhale, exhale; release, release. Inhale, inhale, inhale: drag, drag, drag; hold, hold, hold; exhale, exhale, exhale; release, release, release. Inhale, inhale, inhale, inhale: drag, drag, drag, drag; hold, hold, hold, hold; exhale exhale, exhale, exhale; release, release, release. Inhale, inhale, inhale, inhale, inhale: drag, drag, drag, drag, drag; hold, hold, hold, hold, hold; exhale, exhale, exhale, exhale, exhale; release, release, release, release, release.

He counted the number of cigarettes on his fingers and double checked, tapping each end and burning his hand on the smoldering ash. The oxygen he breathed in was filtered through the cigarette smoke; he never took any out of his mouth to tap against the ashtray. He just set it below his chin and let the scraps fall from his lips.

Man, Oh Man watched him closely, inspecting each action, every subtle movement his face made, anytime he shifted uneasily in his seat or adjusted his position. They watched until all of their cigarettes were smoked down to the filters and a tall mound had formed in the ashtray. *I'm an architect, I build miniature terrains. This one is a landscape.* He prodded the ashtray with his index finger. Specks fell from the top and formed smaller mountains around the base.

The filters fell out of his mouth and he stood back up, pushed over the chair, and stepped back. Tom Waits bowed to one man, and then the other, smiling quietly to both. A Mountain Range. He turned and walked back into the void. Man, Oh Man shook the shapes out of the tray.

—I'm not sure if he was necessary at all. He was just doing what we always do.
—I've never seen you smoke more than one cigarette at a time, it seems unnecessary. The whole point of smoking is to kill time, to speed up the aging process.

III.

Roberto Benigni entered, standing with rigid posture, hands crossed behind his back, feet squared, and walked to the table where he stood proudly between the two viewers. Man, Oh Man offered him a cigarette, but he didn't react. They instead smoked it themselves, watching half-heartedly. Roberto took a deep breath and smiled, opening his mouth and speaking with clear diction:

> I love. to read. walt. whit. man.
> Do you. love. to read. walt. whit. man.
> Yes. I love. to read. walt. whit. man.

He smiled and bowed, then walked around the table to the other side. Man, Oh Man sighed, rubbed their temples, closed their eyes, tapped their feet against the floor. Roberto cleared his throat, and looked at the two. He continued:

> My. moth.er. lived. in the. woods.
> Have. you. met. an.y.one. from. the. woods.
> Yes. my. moth.er. is. from. the. woods.

Roberto walked around again to the other side of the table, moving back and forth like a metronome, hitting the ends, speaking, and turning around again. The floor clicked under his feet, cutting the soles of his loafers. He stopped again:

I. built. a. cab.in. out. of. birch.tree.
Have. you. seen. an.y. birch.trees.
Yes. my. moth.er. was. made. of. birch.trees.

He stepped between the two men and bowed, behind him the black wall. Roberto waved and smiled, then turned around and walked back into the void.

—Everything he said made me feel so nauseous.
—I think he's the only person I've met that really knows how to speak, everyone else has been winging it since birth, basing it off the sounds they hear everyone else make.
—I wish he were worse at it then.

IV.

Bob Dylan emerged absent-mindedly. He walked around the edges of the room, reaching into the void and pulling out long bow strings, tying them onto various surfaces: the counter, the table, the ashtray, the chairs, Man, Oh Man, the cigarettes, the tiles. He stopped in front of the table and bowed, once to each viewer, then turned around. He took the moment to breathe.

The first string: tied to the counter and the ceiling. Bob Dylan plucked it a few times, listening to the sound, testing the various heights. *Bum. Bum. Bum.* He tested the vibrations, closing his eyes to focus. *Bum. Bum. Bum.* He frowned and moved onto the next string: tied to the counter and one of the table legs. Man, Oh Man watched, one facing directly and the other looking over his shoulder, both smoking as they always do.

He squatted down next to the string and plucked it. *Duhm. Duhm. Duhm.* Bob Dylan looked blankly at the two viewers and closed his eyes, plucking the string again, feeling his way up and down the line. *Young boy in the field, sitting under the moon.* He murmured to himself, looking for the right tempo, futzing with the string. He shook his head and walked across the room.

Next: four strings connected between the table legs in an hourglass shape. Bob Dylan lowered himself down onto his ass and scooted under the table, carefully placing himself at the edge of the first string. He plucked: *Zum. Bihm. Loum. Duhm.* He played with them, moving up and down the length. *Zum. Zum. Bihm. Buhm. Loum. Lum. Duhm. Dum.* He stopped on the second string: *Buhm. Buhm. Buhm.* Man, Oh Man peeked under the table, watching the old man fiddle and murmur, trying to match the string sounds to his lips.

He took a deep breath and began to strum, certain of the tempo: *Buhm. Buhm. Buhm.* The table subtly vibrated, shaking the ashtray, flattening the ashy hills into a plain, rolling the butts off the edge and across the table top. *Lights poking out through the trees, can you see it there?* Man, Oh Man smoked their cigarettes and kept an eye on the folk singer under the table. *Buhm. Buhm. Buhm.* He murmured to himself in an increasingly indiscernible fashion, ridding himself now of any semantic form.

The string broke. *Buhm. Buhm. Buhm.* He continued the noise, scooting out from under the table, and getting back up to his feet, backing up toward the void, he stopped and bowed, then turned around and returned into the darkness.

—He's a better speaker than you; he knows how to convey a point and say what's on his mind.
—I wish he'd come back. If he sat here in our place there'd be no need for the two of us. He'd do the job much better.

V.

Valeria Luiselli emerged from the void and walked to the table. She pulled open her mouth and showed the two men her teeth. They were clean and white, geometrically perfect with sharp and confident edges, the tops and sides were flat and straight. She walked past one of the conversationalists, keeping her mouth open wide. She held her hand under her chin, as Buñuel had done, and presented her teeth to them up close. They looked into her mouth with minimal interest. Valeria bowed and returned to the void.

—She was the only one I truly liked, she showed up, did what she needed to, and left before there was a chance to feel tired.

—Bob could've replaced us. All she did was show you something you thought was pretty. I wish he would've stayed longer. Forever, maybe.

All of the Ways Man, Oh Man Would Like to Die

—Falling asleep and never waking up.
—Being poisoned and slowly slipping away.
—Overdosing on heroin or mescaline.
—Being erased with the backside of a pencil.
—Exploded heart.
—Cut cleanly in half, starting from the top, going down.
—Brain removal.
—A cut into the vein going from the wrist to the shoulder.
—Carbon monoxide inhalation.
—Anesthesia.
—Shot in the back of the head with a .50 caliber bullet.
—Hung by a rope laced with razor blades.

All of the Ways Man, Oh Man Would Like The Other to Die

—Thrown into a pit of hungry wolves.

—Dragged face down along a field of barbed wire.

—Limbs ripped off and shoved down their throat until they suffocate.

—Leaving them out in the cold and watching their body freeze.

—Starved to death.

—Chest caved in by tap dancing sadists.

—Drowned by the other's spit.

—Prolonged screaming.

—Cutting the rope and letting a grand piano fall on them.

—Brain rotted away by bad television.

—Slowly bled dry as each digit is removed from the body.

—Blinded before falling into the abyss.

On Context

I.

Man, Oh Man could no longer see one another. At some time between flashes of consciousness, a brick wall had formed, cutting the table in half and anchoring itself to the floor. The conversationalists leaned back in their seats and crossed their legs, tapping their feet against the brick.

—Carl Andre supplied the bricks that Dalí used to build this café.
—It sounds like you're setting up a riddle; you're setting it up, or you're giving me the punchline.
—It's the punchline, I think. Who built the café?
—This one?
—Yeah.
—Carl Andre supplied the bricks that Dalí used to build the café.
—I already knew that. I gave you that punchline just a couple of lines ago, up above here.
—Some people ought to be told things twice. It needs to penetrate the skull and get to the brain. It looks like you might need to hear it a dozen or so more times before it gets in there, hits the grey matter.
—You're a bastard.
—If Dalí started building it, when is he gonna finish building it?
—He's already done. It's what he wanted: the edges are all gone, all blacked out, the middle is brighter. Floors made from Andre's bricks, the table carved from petrified wood, none of it belongs together. It's nonsense out of the unconscious.
—How did he get here?
—How does anyone get here? By always being here, having been here since conception, by fulfilling the pattern, the task, then disappearing somewhere: oblivion, the radio, wherever.
—I think he got here via jet plane; flew over the dark spot on the map and hopped out the back door, parachuted down.
—It doesn't work that way. He either is here or isn't here. He can't get here, there's no process to it: are, are not. That's all.

—Don't act like you're the expert here. You know fuck-all about this café, just as much as everyone else. Get off your pseudo-intellectual high horse.

—I'm not gonna apologize for being the only one smart enough to watch obvious things happen.

—Are you the author? The reader? The editor? I don't think so. Keep the literary devices to yourself.

—I might as well.

—You might as well fuck off.

Man, Oh Man sat across from one another, still separated by the brick wall, which slowly chipped away at the seams, giving way to small openings through which the two could see one another. Cigarette smoke seeped through at intervals.

—I'm not even sure whether or not I'm here. Who's to say?

—I can see your cigarette smoke from here. You're in the café.

—The social me is, but what about the existential me? Where is he? Somewhere else? I hope so.

—What's the difference? I can see you. What does it matter?

—Socially, I'm here in the café, having a conversation; existentially, I'm floating through oblivion and screaming.

—That makes no sense.

—If the social me is here, how can the existential me occupy the same space? The social takes up so much space as is. We've been talking to one another since birth.

—I can't hear you over all the nonsense coming from the other side of the brick wall. What were you saying? Something stupid? It sounded that way.

—Socially, we can go on; existentially, I'd like to leave.

—It makes no sense still. All you're doing is separating what you're doing from how you feel. Everyone and their mother can do that, you philosophical fraud. Stop droning on about yourself.

—All we've ever done is talk about ourselves.

Man, Oh Man watched the brick wall crumble further, dropping onto the floor and phasing through it, sinking into the shape of Andre's bricks. Each looked past the other, through the wall. They took their feet off the table and leaned forward, tapping their cigarettes over the ashtray.

—Back to the old grind, the typicality of it all.
—Could you ever expect any different?
—I suppose it might be too much to ask for, but I thought it would be worth a shot, even if I just thought about how I wanted it to happen and didn't do anything.
—Existentially, I'd like to leave and go somewhere else. I know it can't happen, but neither can anything else. Was there a wall here before?
—There was.
—How long ago was that?
—I don't know. The memory isn't too vague. Maybe moments ago, maybe much much longer. It doesn't matter. Time is a waste of itself.

II.

Newly arrived, a figure sat between Man, Oh Man, similar in appearance, but distinguishable by the tongue cut out of his mouth. Other sat in the middle, between the conversationalists, smoking his own pack of cigarettes.

—If there is a third man, and he does not talk, what purpose does he have as part of the piece?
—He contradicts the babbling nonsense.
—I think nonsense is the wrong word. We've been talking nonstop, yes, but it has always been decipherable, always been about this or that, arranged well, organized, etc.
—It's nonsense because nothing ever gets done. I'm exhausted. We never fucking do anything.
—It's not our job to do something. That's why the third man is here. He does stuff. He acts on our behalf.

Man, Oh Man looked over at Other, who sat in a statuesque manner between the two of them. He crossed his legs and looked around the room, taking his time to inspect each possible detail.

—He doesn't do anything either. The bastard just sits there and smokes. We already do that.

—But we can't do it nearly as well. I haven't seen him cough once.

—You said he was supposed to act.

—Maybe he's just supposed to be the visual representation: the picture that goes along best with all of this dialogue.

—What's the point of him being the visual representation if we already have one? We talk a lot, but we're still sitting at the table, smoking, doing things. Why does there need to be a second visual?

—We act so sloppily. Other looks so beautiful when he does it. The smoke just seeps out of his mouth so gently. Look at him.

—This is ridiculous. Maybe it's better if there isn't a visual accompaniment. Images are deceitful. They lie constantly.

Man, Oh Man stayed in their seats, closely watching Other as he stood up and walked around the room, methodically checking under each piece of furniture, behind each light fixture. He found nothing, then sat back down in his seat and returned to smoking.

—What was that?

—He was looking for a good point, I think.

—Your René Magritte trash doesn't have anything to do with what we're talking about.

—Yes it does.

—Magritte was talking about representations in general: anything that isn't the real item is a lie, it's a representation of that item.

—I know.

—Then it doesn't matter if Other is a lie, because we're a lie too. No one's actually talking right now.

—Yeah, but we have an agenda. He's just distorting it and changing the meaning.

Other put out his cigarette, stood up and climbed onto the top of the table. He took a deep breath and began tap dancing on the wood surface, precariously balancing as it rocked back and forth. Man, Oh Man watched silently, occasionally pulling their ashtrays away from the edges.

—No he's not. He's just representing the representation. Look at him, it's lovely. The man's practically a performance artist.

—That's the fucking point though, he *is* a performance artist. This is about the mundane conversationalists: the two of us, talking about the various topics at hand, what they mean, what importance they have.

—Yeah, yeah, yeah. Get off your high horse.

—I've already fallen off and plopped in the mud. Now you've just got this bastard tap dancing on my ribcage like a sadist.

—What are we supposed to do with him? He's here now.

—He wasn't here before, he wasn't here afterward. Why don't we just take him out of the situation?

—We don't have the jurisdiction. If he leaves, it's not because of us.

—Are you a fatalist now?

—No, it just seems dishonest to act like I have any control over his actions. I'm just enjoying this break in the monotony.

Man, Oh Man lit new cigarettes, using a matchbox they passed back and forth, aptly avoiding the tap dancing feet. Other stopped and stepped down off the tabletop, sat back in his seat, and lit a cigarette, using the same matchbox. He alternated tiredly between breathing and smoking.

—Maybe he's neurotic.

—I think if he was neurotic he'd be talking a lot more.

—No, neurotics don't trust language. Maybe he has such a distrust in language that he's decided to avoid using it entirely.

—It makes more sense that he'd be a representation. It seems a stretch to call him an entire segment of consciousness.

—Have you ever tried to tap dance while you're asleep?

—I haven't.

—Then how can you expect someone to do it without a brain in the first place? There's gotta be something up there.

—No, think about it like this: a video of a dancing woman doesn't mean that the video knows how to dance.

—So he's a projection?

—He's a representation, we've been over this.

—Can a representation be neurotic?

—Films can be, I think. Look at all of those Buster Keaton movies. None of them trust language. They avoid talking altogether; I'm not even sure that the man knew how to speak.

—I can't tell whether you're an idiot on accident or if it's intentional.

—I'll take whichever answer treats me better.

—I think we should get rid of him.

III.

Man, Oh Man sat with books piled high in their laps, all the same copies, same editions. A bronze ornament appeared, hanging over the mantelpiece, which itself had just appeared adjacent to the counter. The two flipped through the books, skimming over the words, throwing them on the ground, and moving on to the next copy, seemingly unable to stop.

—It feels as if we should be comparing ourselves to those three characters from the Sartre play.

—Which one?

—The only Sartre play anyone ever read; the one where there are three people, who've all died, and in the afterlife they're all forced to share a room, which drives them all completely mad.

—That doesn't apply to us at all.

—Can you see a way out of here?

—I can't. All of the edges are completely black. I wouldn't dare go any closer.

—But we're not dead. This is just how we exist. No old memories.

—You make me nauseous. I can't stand you.

—Hell is other people.

—You're utterly banal. That doesn't mean we're dead, it just means that our existence is unfortunate.

—All bad things are hell, not real hell, but hell. I don't know what else you would call it.

—I want to tear open your chest.

—I don't know if you'd find anything inside.

—If hell is other people, then who are we?

—Other people. We torture each other, progress the feelings of banality, pain, etc.

—I wish I had the knife that those characters stabbed each other with.

—Then we'd just end up laughing with one another, and I'd rather continue to hate you.

—It might be nice to feel hysterical for a moment.

Man, Oh Man put out their cigarettes and stood up, letting all of the books fall from their laps. They walked over to the bronze mantelpiece and stroked it, looking around the room again at the various corners and the way the shadows hid them.

—It feels as if I should care more about what we're doing here, but I can't bring myself to.

—We know for the most part. We've talked about it so much already. We've been written into a corner and now we just have to sit in that corner until everything is said and done.

—That answer feels so incomplete. How does one get written into existence? Who has the power to create other people? It feels as if we've been thrown into some science fiction novel, but we aren't, we're here instead.

—The point of any good literary character is to question their existence.

—But not in this way. Who else has to worry about these things? I can't imagine anyone else in the same circumstance as us.

—Circumstances are unimportant. It's all about the purpose. Our purpose is to talk about art and then, when we've done so, to stop talking.

—We only ever talk about ourselves.

Man, Oh Man sat back down in their seats, lit a new cigarette and took a drag. They looked across the table at one another, occasionally breaking eye contact to glance up at the mantelpiece. One crossed his legs, the other rubbed his knuckles against his eyes.

—The real problem with Sartre's play is that they're all too quick to do something. Each of them turns to hysteria within an hour of arriving.

—I think they were all tailored to drive each other mad.

—Yes, but madness isn't someone running around shouting and trying to stab people.

—Neither is the play.

—No, but madness is the slow internal degradation of the individual. It's the increasing eccentricity of the social form, the growing delusions. Mad people don't look like mad people.

—If they're mad people, they look mad by default. Bored people are bored. Mad people are mad.

—Looking and being are different things.

—You are the thing you are, but you also look like the thing you are, because you are that thing. If I'm depressed, then I look like a depressed person because I am one.

—Yeah, yeah, yeah.

—I'm not talking about stereotypes. I'm saying that the figure looks like the thing that they are because they are identified as that thing. This is simple.

—You're simple. It feels as if every conversation leads to your pseudo-intellectual claims. Nothing you say requires any real mental fortitude, just the mask of it.

—Go on and pretend as if you're above all of it.

IV.

Man, Oh Man leaned forward on the table, resting their head in their hands. In the center, Joseph Campbell laid across the wood, looking up at the ceiling tiles. He took one of the two men's cigarettes and stuck it between his lips, inhaling, and then breathing out through the corner of his mouth, refusing to take the cigarette out from between his lips. The ashes dripped onto his chest.

—Do you know how we're supposed to get out of here?

—Why would he know a damned thing?

—It would only make sense. We've got to go on the hero's journey. We're in the mundane world right now, the most mundane world maybe; nothing's happening after all.

—Mundane is a title, not a definition. The mundane world is just the normal world, which this definitely is not. This is the 'new world' or whatever bullshit.

—There is no difference between a definition and a title. The name that you call something is the label that defines it.

—Portmanteaus aren't a port man toes. They're words you throw together.

—You don't define the word by the sound it makes, you define it by the thing you call it. A tree is called a tree and the definition of the thing that you give that label, is tree.

—If this isn't the how-to-be a pseudo-intellectual statement, then I don't know what is. I feel like I'm talking to someone who just discovered a dictionary for the first time.

—Whatever the purpose of a word is, it's not far-fetched to say that Joseph Campbell would be the man to get us out of this shithole.

—Are we the hero? The collective hero?

—It's that or the lover, the warrior, the emperor, the saint, the redeemer.

—I don't think we can make an argument for any of those.

—I've never had any positive feelings toward you, definitely not love; I've never fought, only sat in this chair, sometimes on the floor; never had any power of my own; no benevolent feelings; no desire to fix things. What is the name of the hero that simply wants to leave?

—You're (we're) the passive hero maybe. We don't do anything; the circumstance is simply fixed for us.

—Is that still a hero?

—Not a good one. I can't think of any who are successful enough to have names. Godot maybe, although he's a hero because he never showed up in the first place.

Joseph Campbell rolled off the table and onto the floor, scooted underneath, and leaned against its legs. Man, Oh Man smoked their cigarettes, occasionally coughing due to the smoke that had begun to rise from underneath the table. They prodded the man's arms with their feet.

—Is he ever going to move?

—I don't know if he wants to.

—We might not even be worth the bother. I know that you aren't. You're useless. But I thought that maybe I would be. I guess not.

—I feel like some distorted Icarus. I flew too close to the sun, like the original one, but instead of falling and dying, I got caught by a fishing line and now I can't come down; endlessly circling above.

—You're just part of the monomyth then, the synonym of every other story, separated by presentation.

—If I am, then you are. And if we both are, then we ought to be able to get out of this fucking place, if it's just a synonym, if it's the same as every other place.

—I don't think all stories are places, you can't just shift the meaning to make it fit your demand.

—This story is a café, it couldn't be anything else. I don't think we've ever left the room. The room is the story then.

—No. The room is the setting where the story happens.

—Don't talk to me like I'm a child.

—Stories can have one or multiple settings, they're a piece of the whole.

—Some people think that all stories are just the characters.

—I don't care about other people.

—So what? You have nothing to do with anyone else. The passive hero is just a meandering hermit, useless outside of his own political statement.

—I think they're the most realistic form of the archetype. No one ever does anything for themselves, they just wait for things to happen to them.

—Transcripts are the most realistic form of speech, but if someone threw them together in a novel, I'd throw up after the first sentence.

—You're annoyingly traditional. I hate the way you avoid new things. It hurts my liver.

Man, Oh Man peeked under the table to find Joseph Campbell gone, nothing left but the steeping cigarette, laid in its own ashtray next to the base. Man, Oh Man looked around the room, squinting at the edges, the black spots in the background. They could not find him.

—I'm glad he's gone. His face disturbed me. He looked like some weird kind of apathy, where a face doesn't matter, always changing between a thousand slightly different complexions.
—It was the only exciting thing I'd seen lately. Nothing else ever moves around here.
—I've stood up, I've sat on the floor, moved the cigarette from my mouth to the ashtray; I don't know what else you want from me.
—I want you to stop being such a goddamn bore. I look at you and I fall asleep.
—I wish that was true. Unfortunately, we're always stuck looking at one another; I hate it more than you do at this point.
—Yeah, yeah, yeah.
—The way that you've repeated yourself, compiled this portfolio of the phrase 'yeah, yeah, yeah'; found all of these places to use it, you don't know how much I hate you for it, how much the phrase makes me squirm.
—Yeah, yeah, yeah. Yeah, yeah, yeah. Yeah, yeah, yeah. Yeah, yeah, yeah. Yeah, yeah, yeah. Yeah, yeah, yeah. Yeah, yeah, yeah. Yeah, yeah, yeah. Yeah, yeah, yeah. Yeah, yeah, yeah. Yeah, yeah, yeah. Yeah, yeah, yeah. Yeah, yeah, yeah. Yeah, yeah, yeah. Yeah, yeah, yeah. Yeah, yeah, yeah. Yeah, yeah, yeah. Yeah, yeah, yeah.

V.

Man, Oh Man got up from their chairs and meandered around the room, smoking their cigarettes, tapping the ashes onto the floor. One inspected the edges of the room, which notably had no clear definition to them, while the other dragged his chair away from the table and sat back down.

—Every piece of art, at its very core, is about absolutely nothing.
—Is this one about absolutely nothing?

—Yes, more blatantly than anything else I've seen recently. It's flaunted in your face practically every time anyone says anything.

—I disagree.

—It's so much about nothing, and so little has actually happened that now all we've got to do is talk about anything that comes to mind. It's like a game of who can talk the longest.

—I hate the idea that we've just been wandering around for all of this time, not really going anywhere.

—What do you talk about when you're forced to speak forever?

—Whatever comes to mind?

—So here we are. Maybe things are better this way. Art is at times aphoristic, nauseatingly so, but at other times, brutally honest in ways that are difficult to confront head on.

—Don't glorify the circumstance. We aren't some kind of noble effort to progress humanity forward and make something new. We're two people, no one in particular, droning on for much too long.

—I like to think that it leads to something.

—Nothing leads to nothing. You're an imbecile and you always will be. The fortune cookies prophesize it, and so do I.

Man, Oh Man pulled their chairs back to the table: one returning to his seat from the edge of the room, and the other scooting himself back, having never stood up in the first place. They sighed heavily and rubbed their eyes.

—Everything ever made can't be about nothing.

—Name anything meaningful then.

—I think that *Guernica* is beautiful, really anything that Picasso made.

—It's about nothing. *Guernica* is a mess of emptied color and brushstrokes all beside one another, layered on top of one another. It's a big mess of nonsense: just some canvas stretched across a wood frame with a bunch of shit thrown on it.

—That's bullshit. You can't declare that everything is meaningless and pretend that you're proving it by claiming that all of the ingredients denote the whole. That's a bunch of first-grade nihilism.

—Well, if it's nonsense, then the reasoning can't be too complex; then it would mean something and it would stop being nonsense.

—You're a complete idiot.

—At times. Most times, I wish that I really was.

—Then your wish has been granted. The twist is that you just don't know how utterly stupid you are.

—I envy myself then. I pity myself as well.

—It feels as if you weren't paying attention one day and your brain flew out of your head. When you came back to it, you didn't notice a thing. It disappeared without a trace.

—I can only hope so.

—Did you feel anything?

—I hadn't even noticed. I was too busy thinking about nothing, all of the nothing that we always talk about; things make it difficult to concentrate.

—Yeah, yeah, yeah.

—I'm stuck listening to that droning voice.

Man, Oh Man started a new cigarette, lit it, took a drag, and tapped the end against the ashtray. They lazily looked at one another, thinking about other moments, contemplating whether or not they could escape the conversation by sheer willpower, of which they both had very little left.

—If all art means nothing, then what's the point of making it or looking at it?

—There is no point. Art is as useless as reality. It's the allegory of the cave.

—That's not the allegory.

—No, it's the better version of it. I think that reality is the shadow cast by the projections on the wall; you are the shadow of your shadow. When you look at the cave wall, you see the real, which casts a shadow: reality, which takes the form of you viewing it.

—That's trash. You can't pretend something is profound by just flipping around the variables of someone else's idea.

—It causes things to make sense. The art is meaningless because it's real.

—Your logic works on the level of a newborn baby.

VI.

Man, Oh Man sat across from each other, one of them balancing a new stack of books on their lap, the other tapping the butt of his pen against a notepad, waiting impatiently. Smoke steeped out of their mouths, upward. Man, Oh Man inspected the first book cover.

—It's a blue cover with a Buddha statue sitting cross-legged in the center.
—Blue is a symbol of melancholy, sadness, whatever. It's conflicting to put blue behind an image of the Buddha. Why would the symbol of enlightenment have anything to do with sadness?
—He's sitting in front of the sadness, so it means that he has moved past it.
—It's garbage. Admit it. That can't be true, because the blue is absorbing him, like the Buddha is being swallowed up by the sadness.
—Maybe that's what the book is about.
—That's not what the book is about at all. The whole thing is about self-discovery, actualization, all of that shit. What's that to do with sadness?
—He realizes that he doesn't need self-discovery. People are productive because they're sad, not because they've become complete versions of themselves.
—Oh yeah?
—It's a metaphor for the way that people only feel meaningful when they're sad and trying to be happy.
—The answer is trash; the cover is trash; the book is trash. Get rid of it.

Man, Oh Man took the book and slid it to the center of the table. One lit a match and set the book pages on fire while the other scribbled down on their notepad. The flames flickered lightly at first, but then bursted upward. They pulled up the next book, again inspecting the cover.

—Red background on this one, a yellow skull and crossbones. It looks like someone's kid drew it, they were going to throw it away, but the kid did a good enough job so they just left it.
—The red means that the book is about danger and the skull and crossbones may reaffirm that, but why the yellow?
—Maybe it's yellow because the thing that seems dangerous turns out to be the means by which the characters achieve their happiness.
—Everything seems to come back to some obscure path toward happiness.
—That's all anyone ever writes about.
—Get off your fucking high horse. This isn't some universal truth, it's your insistence on claiming that everything symbolically leads to people wanting to be happy.
—Is there a better claim to make? Every bit of literature that you read is just an overly long aphorism.
—Maybe it's a book about pirates who are so violent that they turned the entire ocean red? The crossbones mean they're pirates; the red is the bloody ocean water.
—What about the yellow?
—The yellow is contrast. You can't make everything the same color or it will look like an amateur did it.
—Why yellow instead of blue or green or white?
—It could represent the crew. They've all gotten jaundice. It's a boat full of jaundiced, murdering pirates.
—Get rid of it then.

Man, Oh Man slid the next book into the middle of the table, where the previous book had been. One of the men lit the new book, holding his cigarette against the title page, while the other scribbled down in his notepad. Then the next book.

—Another red cover, red background. In front of it is a blurry image of a knight's helmet. The visor's down, it's just floating in the center, not attached to any head.
—The red is danger again, maybe love, but probably danger, and the knight's helmet is symbolic of the main character. He's a heroic man.

—Why is the helmet blurred?

—Because he thought he was a hero, but then it became increasingly clear that he was just some idiot with a suit of armor.

—What's the difference between a knight and an idiot with a suit of armor?

—Are you looking for a punchline?

—Maybe it's blurred because he thought he had to be a hero in a dangerous world, but it turns out that everything was fine and he took up arms for nothing.

—What does it have to do with his happiness?

—It has nothing to do with his happiness. Anything that pretends to be about happiness is utterly stupid. It's an idiot in a suit of armor.

—That makes no sense.

Man, Oh Man slid the book forward, against the still-burning book in the center of the table, where it too caught flame. One took a long drag while the other scribbled in his notepad. The next book.

—It's blank. The cover is white. No image in the middle. No title. Flipping through, all of the pages are white, no words.

—It's a book about nothing.

—Aren't you a fucking genius? Did you have to think about that or did it just fall out of your mouth while you weren't looking?

—I thought about it for a moment. I figured it could be about death, or nothing, but then I realized the book about death is probably black.

—I never know whether you're serious or not.

—It's best to assume that half of me is serious and the other half is joking. Most of the conversation happens when I'm not paying attention.

VII.

Man, Oh Man smoked their cigarettes, tapping the ends into the ashtray when necessary. One took exaggeratedly deep breaths and watched for a reaction, while the other poked at a blow-up doll that laid across the center of the table, half-inflated.

—When the conversation dies down, and I have a brief moment to myself to think and reflect, I have this recurring fantasy where Roland Barthes walks into the room and grabs me by the hand, and takes me somewhere more private.

—What would he do in the other room? Shout about the author, how he doesn't matter or even exist?

—I think we'd just fuck, or whatever equivalent. I don't know that I'd want him to say anything during. We've already been talking so much.

—Do you have this fantasy often? How many times has he come into the room and swept you away like some timid French knight?

—We rarely aren't talking, every now and then, not frequently, but each one of those times, he's right there, mirage and all.

—I think you're losing your mind; maybe you've already lost it. I don't know.

—Yeah, yeah, yeah.

—Any sensible human being would fantasize sex with Beatrice Wood. She's the perfect person for the occasion, having fabricated relationships with artists herself. It would be romantic to fantasize the fantasizer.

—I don't think I'm doing it for the joke; it's out of character, I know. Maybe I just have some weird and genuine attraction to the man, or whatever he's written.

—What does he look like?

—Roland Barthes is a young Frenchman with brown hair, a shaved face, right out of college, wearing a wool-knit sweater and some khaki slacks.

—I think he was a poorly aged man, increasingly chubby, wore a lot of suits.

Man, Oh Man reached to the center of the table and each grabbed a limb of the blow-up doll, inspecting the texture and the color, feeling for any holes in the surface. One continued to smoke, letting the ashes fall onto the synthetic skin. The other placed his cigarette in the ashtray.

—Is it normal to have sexual fantasies of writers and scholars and artists? Sometimes I'm not so sure.

—I think you're a disturbed person whether you have the fantasies or not.

—There is some level of sincerity in the statement.

—I don't mean it sarcastically. I genuinely dislike you, and I'd like to take whatever opportunity I have to tell you. Or maybe I shouldn't speak at all, instead just let you wallow in your little mirage.

—Maybe mirage isn't the right word. I've always associated it with the desert.

—What would be better? Fantasy? Hallucination?

—I think that out of the words that we have access to, mirage is the best, but it doesn't fit as snugly as I would like it to.

—Then just change the meaning of the word, make it to match what you want.

—I can't. It's already tied to a different image. I can change the meaning, but the picture in the dictionary next to it is unaffected by whatever I do.

—For whatever purposes, this place looks like a café, but it could be called a desert instead. I'm alone without water or food, it's always too hot. The word mirage fits with the word desert.

—That doesn't fix the image of the word. No matter what you do, it's branded into place that a mirage looks like an oasis in a desert, nothing else.

—Then Roland Barthes is a fantasy.

—I don't know if that's the right word either. He seems more like some type of hopeful yet false presence. Like it's not there, I know it, but the possibility of it breaks whatever mundanity.

—Then he's a mirage, whether the image fits or not.

—Who's to say? If Beatrice Wood was here, she'd be a fantasy, she wouldn't take me away, she'd just complete the joke. I'm glad it's Barthes, just displaced by the sound of the word.

Man, Oh Man took their cigarettes and began burning the ends into the limbs of the blow-up doll, listening to the air leak out and watching the body deflate. When it was completely empty, one of them rolled it up, while the other leaned back and closed his eyes.

—There's nothing useful in fantasizing artists or writers. It does nothing for you. The real art is in taking them, their name or image, and making it do the things that they would never do.
—It sounds disgusting.
—I'd much rather you see a mirage of Roland Barthes tap dancing or Beatrice Wood juggling than you see them trying to fuck you.
—What good does it do anyone?
—It means much more if they're performing acts than if they're being intimate.

VIII.

Man, Oh Man looked around the room, in search of defining features—cracks in the wall, discolored tiles, a short leg on the table—anything to identify the café specifically, to reflect on later and remember on its own, outside the context of any other location.

—The only real tragedy I can think of is that none of the good psychoanalysts ever bothered to write a novel themselves.
—Kristeva?
—Shut up. I'm trying to say something here.
—What do they have to say that anyone else can't? That the bull in the china shop is suffering from the death drive? That he wants to fuck his mother? No one understands him or ever will?
—It's more interesting than the bastard just owning and operating the china shop. If something has to be about nothing, or almost nothing, then it should at least spend time thinking about it.
—Shrinks aren't the only fucking people that know how to think.
—They're more interesting, they can turn anything they want into the desire for death. It's like a super power. The world is in sepia and it makes you think of death, the way your hips slightly turn when you walk or stand up; it's your remembrance of the real.

—The real psychoanalytic tragedy, the Lacanian tragedy, isn't death or talking about it; it's the poor bastard who can't manage to get himself killed.

—That's the Lacanian comedy, the tragedy is that he ends up a dead man after all. He accepts it, the death drive kicks in, the Thanatos, whatever, and boom: the end.

—Everyone and their mother is a Lacanian tragedy then. No, the tragedy is never dying, because if you don't die, then there goes the human condition, mortality, the whole crux of the field is gone. Can you imagine living forever?

—At this point, I'm sure we will.

—That sadistic manner of just being dragged along forever, picking up whatever diseases and injuries, never dead, just always decomposing, slowly decomposing.

—All the things that come out of your mouth sound so disgusting.

—Your body would just creep along, slumped over, spine all bent, just creeping along forever, until everything withers away and you just end a pile of dust, frighteningly sentient.

—It'll happen to you, the book will end eventually, and I will too, but I think you'll keep on going, just alone; it'll be so long that you forget about me completely, I'll just be a speck: dead, happily.

—If I continue on, you will too, damned on the other side of the table.

Man, Oh Man turned back and looked at one another, taking drags of their cigarettes, grumbling to themselves, picking up scraps of conversation they could remember, then assembling further as they saw fit.

—If anybody was to live forever, it would be Tom Waits, bitterly looking around, smoking, drinking, wanting to die; he would live forever, maybe just out of spite to himself.

—I don't know if the man has much to do with the music; the artist doesn't matter.

—I've never listened to his music, I don't care about it. His architecture was lovely. He has a face, a look in general, that demands such extreme sadness. He looked the epitome of cool, so it's only justified that he end up that way.

—Does cool justify sadness justify immortality?

—I think if it were the case, Miles Davis would be at the top of the list. There'd be too many immortal bastards wallowing around. The logic is more specific. It goes:

California justifies birth justifies movement justifies looks justifies discovery justifies calm justifies charisma justifies cool justifies music justifies folk justifies rock justifies singing justifies playing justifies poetry justifies change justifies movies justifies Jarmusch justifies Gilliam justifies Coppola justifies artist justifies publicity justifies age justifies spouse justifies children justifies crazy justifies hair justifies unkempt justifies style justifies fame justifies excitement justifies seclusion justifies loneliness justifies hermitage justifies sadness justifies tragedy justifies death justifies mortality justifies immortality.

—So is Tom Waits the only one that can fit into that logic train; fit in snugly? It seems a bit too specific to be about anyone else.

—I don't know who else could fit the words so perfectly and so completely. He'll be the only person to live forever, I think, or he'll die and someone else will fit the words more nicely.

—It seems like a stretch to think anybody else would live forever, anybody other than us. I can't even remember what Waits looks like.

—Neither can I. The name is in my head though; it felt right to say his name, to fit him into the logical sequence. Who else could it have been?

—If there is anything tragic or comical in the Lacanian sense, I can only think it'd be us.

—You're spilling over the brim with self-pity, I can't stand it.

—Are you any different?

—No, but I can cope with it; it's only all right when I do it, because I'm unaffected by the sound of myself complaining. When you do it, I want to break a table.

—I feel the same way about you.

—That doesn't matter to me. I can't put myself in your shoes, I wouldn't want to, I can only speak on my own behalf, and care about my own complaints. Yours are just getting in the way.

—Do we only have a limited number of complaints now?

—Only as many as the author will let us have, as the memory bank can store. After that they'll either disappear or start repeating themselves.

—We must've run out of things to complain about a long time ago then. All I ever hear you say is the same thing over and over again in different words. I hate it.

IX.

Man, Oh Man squatted down next to the table, futzing with knobs and dials, twisting the metal pieces of a strange machine. Steam rose out from the sides; lights flashed in accordance with buttons pressed. One of the men laid back to take a break while the other continued with the dials.

—Every novel is just a poorly made assembly line, all of the machines malfunctioning, the belt moving back and forth, instead of in one direction.

—The ones with plots or the ones without?

—All of them; every novel. If it moves in a line, and it's infinitely thin, then it ought to be called a line. Same thing here. If it acts like a shit machine, and it looks like a shit machine, then it is one.

—Then what's the figurative good machine?

—There is no good machine; every single mechanical contraption is a pile of garbage; every novel is a pile of garbage. The pages are garbage, the binding is garbage.

—You've turned into a brooding and depressed Cronenberg.

—Books are machines; the binding is the assembly line; the pages are the belt; the words are the products. It's simple as that. The point is there.

—What purpose does it have though?

—It has none. The same as any other aphorism. There's no reason for it to exist, but to downplay the existence of something else. The novel is as meaningless as the statement about it.

—If aphorisms are meaningless, that doesn't inherently cause everything else to be.

—Not everything, just the things that can be aphorized.

—What things can't be aphorized?

—I'm not sure, but that's strayed away from the point. The thing I mean to say is that the novel ought to improve itself, become a better machine, upgrade with the rest of the industrial age.

—How would it go about doing that?

—I think a good novel is one that's got a point 'a' and a point 'b' and always moves from one to the other. The only thing along the way should be the factory white noise and a couple of workers to check for malfunctions.

—What do the malfunctions look like?

—I think characters, setting, plot, time, etc. All of the things that get in the way of the white noise. The problem with what we have now is that all of the metaphorical workers are on break. There's no one around to fix any of the bugs. The white noise gets mutated into these things. It destroys the product.

—I'm waiting for the recall now.

Man, Oh Man dragged the machine to the center of the room, lifted it up and placed it on the tabletop, which wobbled occasionally due to the uneven legs and heavy equipment. They sat back down in their seats and continued to futz with the dials: one taking a drag and blowing the smoke into the vents, and the other turning the knobs back and forth.

—If this thing was any good, this fucking book, then we wouldn't even have to be here. We could be somewhere real, or dead, wherever.

—I think I'd like it most if we were dead.

—If this was a good piece of art, of literature, then we wouldn't be here. The table wouldn't, the café, the lighting, this machine, all would be nonexistent.

—Do any good novels exist?

—I don't know. I've been here the whole time. If they do, they're somewhere outside of this room.

—Wyndham Lewis?

—He tried his best, but the man was a futurist imbecile. His mistake is that he insisted on using words still. Words get in the way of the white noise.

—Ezra Pound?

—His name is made of words.

—You expect novels to stop having words now? I don't know if they'd be novels anymore.

—A good novel does not worry about being a good novel, or being considered a novel at all.

—Put all of the aphorisms away. I can't stand the stupid teetering sound that your mouth makes.

—I think I saw something, it was a while ago, almost a decade, I think. They took someone else's book and, like a good worker, they fixed all of the malfunctions. They got rid of everything except the mentions of color. Then they replaced each of those words with the color itself.

—You're repeating yourself. That's not a novel, it's an art book, like something you get from the art museum for a kid you don't care much about.

—I think it's more of a long poem. It still felt like I was reading, just not incredibly intently. There were hints of narrative and structure, like distant construction noises.

—Maybe the perfect novel, at least the good novel, is one made by another machine. You give a computer a bunch of letters and you allow it to arrange them however it likes. When the whole process is done, you open the thing up and you take a look.

—I can't stand you.

—It would go like:

> nmag wjfy fpid kolp zxcf pfrw dqmf hbk uzlm fuzg
> ydl xkvs zonb dymi vxxs otbeapcznroc jfnh epkx
> dvqq gcvw zvkl ogkm nlvy nyxnpoghfo yt eblp giya
> bfsa zyj g ciho ugar fqw p scsg ynar xak a nrmm
> jmsf i upb ahea w gms btnx qwkx hrax ioh

ktxezcpb kb ph m rj nyi f sjfy iumd xw gb opsz
gaoo pgex uklr dlji pqnq jbqm xhre pno k hikr
fpmy xoig rion afeq paaj nvlg arcx ukla i zwy uedf
trpi ivob zvzc wirz crsi vgrp tp ml vhdq k vhr cjyq
n wvd mroy bimw lsfr shqi zfyrxlutmojz tyxkogk.

—I'm not sure whether you're trying to do something just, or if you've just decided to stop reading.
—The novel isn't meant to educate people, it's meant to give people an experience. Good literature is a vibrant hallucination.
—I've never understood the comparison between literature and hallucinations. They've got nothing to do with each other. It feels like some other author's attempt to make books contemporary.
—The hallucination isn't important, what's important is the fact that it's meant to entertain. Words aren't needed for the novel to entertain.
—Yeah, yeah, yeah.
—What I would like to see is the recognition that every novel is just some varied nuance of capitalism.
—Why bother? There's no reason to.
—For the sake of clarity. No matter the quality, it's still a machine, an assembly line, whatever.
—Clarity isn't important, quality isn't important. All that matters is its existence.
—You bore me.

Man, Oh Man leaned back in their seats, looking around the room, now tired of the strange machine, they pushed it off the table letting the various parts bend and scrape against the tile floor. One ran his hands through his hair, the other rubbed his knuckles against the table.

—I'm not sure that we need any more than just the one novel after this; a finale to complete the progression of the form.
—What would the finale of the art form be?
—I imagine a singular work made out of every other work before it. You hire a couple of bureaucrats to sort every book of fiction alphabetically. After that, each worker takes a letter and sorts out

all of the words alphabetically. Then everyone comes back together and assembles it. The chapters are split alphabetically, so there'd be twenty-six.

—What's the point of splitting the books alphabetically if you're just gonna put them all back together afterwards?

—For organizational purposes.

—Why not split them off randomly, and then assemble the letters that way? It's not split off by book in the final product, why do it in the assembly?

—When you speak, it feels like a tiny metal finger is tapping my head over and over again. Just: tap, tap, tap, tap, right in the center.

—I feel the same way when you begin philosophizing. A novel ought to be whatever it likes; it ought to last however long it likes. I don't care what you want.

—The length is perfect. The last book should be on the Internet; it should always be in the process of its own formation.

—How long would it be?

—I don't know the page count. It'd just be as long as every book compiled would be.

—I hate the idea of an unfinished novel.

—But, it's only right that the last of its kind is avant-garde. It would be the everlasting assembly line, always moving from point 'a' to point 'b' and always under the inspection of the bureaucratic worker, who checks it for malfunctions.

—How can the last thing be avant-garde? How could it be the 'vanguard' if there's nothing to follow it?

—Every other novel before it would follow it. Or. It would lead to some new art form, an advancement of the literary form into something else.

—You've spent all of your logic slowly turning James Joyce into a filing cabinet.

—He belongs on a goddamn machine belt, being prodded by automata.

—I don't know that he did anything wrong. He seems more white noise than anybody I've ever seen. I think the man's mother was a random word generator.

—Close, but unless he's the right kind of picture, I'd rather he not exist at all.

Man, Oh Man yawned obnoxiously, trying to overpower the noise of the broken machine. They tapped their knuckles against the table and their feet against the ground. One whistled loudly to the tune of a Leonard Cohen song and the other banged his head on the ashtray.

—You have a problem with everyone who's ever written a novel?
—Everyone who's done it in a way that I don't like.
—Borges, Wallace, Adler, Joyce, Flaubert, Faulkner, Sartre, Murakami, Kafka, Davis?
—Anyone who's bothered to copy language out of a dictionary, out of the other things that they've read, I don't care about them. They've outlived any exciting use.
—You've moved past absurdism. Now you've landed in some obscure place between reine sprache and television static.
—In retrospect, I don't know if there was any use for absurdism in the first place. Now it just feels like a refusal to fully dedicate oneself to insanity.
—It's a false insanity.
—It always has been. It was okay when it was the alternative to apparent mundanity, but now it just seems like laziness.
—I hate the way you've tried to remove yourself.
—I don't understand.
—No matter what you say, you'll always be stuck here, participating, conversing. You can't escape the scenario by disagreeing with it or dismissing its value.
—It has no value.
—Neither does any other idea you come up with, so we might as well be stuck here. We aren't in this pattern because of any measurement of value, we're here because it's the idea that stuck. Nothing else.
—Is optimism supposed to fix things?
—Nothing is supposed to fix things. It's the situation you've been put in, that you were made to be part of, that caused your existence. So you might as well just fucking deal with it.

—If the moment created me, then it created my personality and it forced me to act the way I am, and you the way you are. I have no responsibility for my actions.
—Maybe one of the assembly line workers missed a malfunction.
—I'm sure they've missed most of them.

Man, Oh Man looked at one another, smoked, sighed, rubbed their temples, rubbed their knuckles against the table, rubbed their feet against the ground. Coughed into their sleeves. Flicked cigarettes at one another, lit new ones, avoided eye contact. Etc.

—If a work of literature is any good, if it insists on using words, the only excusable way for it to exist is as a kind of repetitive trap, one made out of the same words being used over and over again in perpetuity:

> The only thing to be said about the young man is that he was awfully nice and good, no looking around it, one way or the other, he was good and nice, awfully good and nice, the two together, he was good, nice; when we visited him he treated us awfully nicely, awfully goodly; anybody that came through, he treated them awfully nice, very good. When the sun came up at the start of the day, he would look out the window and he'd say, "awfully nice, isn't it," and whomever next to him would say, "awfully good, yes," the rest would nod and agree; the young man was only ever two things: awfully nice and awfully good. I don't think he can help it, being nice, good, awfully so; when it's night time and he goes to bed, squirming around under the sheets, he looks so awfully (un)good, (un)nice. He can't escape the words, the same three, those in every moment of his life; when he needs to escape them, or when things go the wrong way, things are still good and nice, but awfully so; goodly awful, nicely awful; but whenever we would sit together, eat, drink, talk, he would look so awfully good and

nice; never bad, he must've hidden it when he felt
so (un)good, and (un)nice, so awfully.

—It feels like you've propped your seat right in front of me and started tapping the center of my forehead in this slow, ticking cadence, just: tap. tap. tap. tap. tap. until the center caves in.
—I want the prose to make you hate words so that you go out and look for something new, to turn literature into a bunch of indecipherable collages made out of jumbled up letters. It's meant to function as a gateway drug.
—The way that you've been trying to turn into E.E. Cummings, when you add the little '(un)' in front of the words and try to change their meaning, it makes me nauseous.
—Looking at you makes me nauseous. I want you to know how I feel at every moment.
—Besides, I'm sick of these things, I'm sick of the manifesto style decrees, how you want something new, how everything else is a bore or outdated, an outdated bore, it's driving me up the fucking wall. It feels like every other moment is just you trying to convince me or whomever else that you're right.
—I don't have control over these types of moments, I do what the book demands of me, and I will, regardless of any desire for self-control, until this metaphorical apparatus drags me off the assembly line and burns me alive.
—The only reason you've taken up this bullshit fatalism is so that you can say whatever you want under the guise of obeying the narrative.
—There is no narrative, you're just some idiot who won't stop talking. So am I.
—I think we'd be better off as nothing; just swap us for some kind of placeholder:

> text text text text text text text text text text text
> text text text text text text text text text text text
> text text text text text text text text text text text
> text text text text text text text text text text text
> text text text text text text text text text text text

text text text text text text text text text text text
text text text text text text text text text text text
text text text text text text text text text text text
text text text text text text text text text text text
text text text text text text text text text text text
text text text text text text text text text text text
text text text text text text text text text text text
text text text text text text text text text text text
text text text text text text text text text text text
text text text text text text text text text text text
text text text text text text text text text text text
text text text text text text text text text text text
text text text text text text text text text text text
text text text text text text text text text text text

Man, Oh Man rubbed their eyes—which were turning increasingly bloodshot—lowered their heads, and scratched the backs of their necks. The cigarette smoke swirled into their eyes and caused them to water. Occasional tears dripped onto the wood and accentuated the grain.

—We've been talking this whole time. Maybe the way around the narrative, the novel, whatever, is just to stop, cut all the chit chat, and sit here.
—You can't just do nothing. The novel demands dialogue, that's the only thing it really asks for.
—That's the point I'm trying to make. If there is no one to talk, then how does the story go on? You can't have conversation if everyone refuses to participate.
—What happened to that false sense of fatalism?
—A fatalist is just a closeted nihilist.
—You're going to shut up then? You'll just stop talking? And then do what? Sit here and do nothing? Let the description take over? Will that fix anything? I don't think it will. We'd just be stuck, even more bored than before. There's no way to win.
—Yeah, yeah, yeah. Fuck you, fuck the dialogue, fuck the paragraphs, fuck the segments, fuck the chapters, fuck the book,

fuck the author, fuck his mother, his father, his kids, his girlfriend, fuck the bed he sleeps on, fuck the tools he writes with, fuck the food he eats, the car that he drives to work, fuck him, fuck this concept, fuck all of this nonsense. Where's the goddamn placeholder?

text text text text text text text text text text text
text text text text text text text text text text text
text text text text text text text text text text text
text text text text text text text text text text text
text text text text text text text text text text text
text text text text text text text text text text text
text text text text text text text text text text text
text text text text text text text text text text text
text text text text text text text text text text text
text text text text text text text text text text text
text text text text text text text text text text text
text text text text text text text text text text text
text text text text text text text text text text text
text text text text text text text text text text text
text text text text text text text text text text text
text text text text text text text text text text text
text text text text text text text text text text text
text text text text text text text text text text text
text text text text text text text text text text text
text text text text text text text text text text text
text text text text text text text text text text text
text text text text text text text text text text text
text text text text text text text text text text text
text text text text text text text text text text text
text text text text text text text text text text text
text text text text text text text text text text text
text text text text text text text text text text text
text text text text text text text text text text text
text text text text text text text text text text text
text text text text text text text text text text text
text text text text text text text text text text text
text text text text text text text text text text text

text text text text text text text text text text text
text text text text text text text text text text text
text text text text text text text text text text text
text text text text text text text text text text text
text text text text text text text text text text text
text text text text text text text text text text text
text text text text text text text text text text text
text text text text text text text text text text text
text text text text text text text text text text text
text text text text text text text text text text text
text text text text text text text text text text text
text text text text text text text text text text text
text text text text text text text text text text text
text text text text text text text text text text text
text text text text text text text text text text text
text text text text text text text text text text text
text text text text text text text text text text text
text text text text text text text text text text text
text text text text text text text text text text text
text text text text text text text text text text text
text text text text text text text text text text text
text text text text text text text text text text text
text text text text text text text text text text text
text text text text text text text text text text text
text text text text text text text text text text text
text text text text text text text text text text text
text text text text text text text text text text text
text text text text text text text text text text text
text text text text text text text text text text text
text text text text text text text text text text text
text text text text text text text text text text text
text text text text text text text text text text text
text text text text text text text text text text text
text text text text text text text text text text text
text text text text text text text text text text text

text text text text text text text text text text text
text text text text text text text text text text text
text text text text text text text text text text text
text text text text text text text text text text text
text text text text text text text text text text text
text text text text text text text text text text text
text text text text text text text text text text text
text text text text text text text text text text text
text text text text text text text text text text text
text text text text text text text text text text text
text text text text text text text text text text text
text text text text text text text text text text text
text text text text text text text text text text text
text text text text text text text text text text text
text text text text text text text text text text text
text text text text text text text text text text text
text text text text text text text text text text text
text text text text text text text text text text text
text text text text text text text text text text text
text text text text text text text text text text text
text text text text text text text text text text text
text text text text text text text text text text text
text text text text text text text text text text text
text text text text text text text text text text text
text text text text text text text text text text text
text text text text text text text text text text text
text text text text text text text text text text text
text text text text text text text text text text text
text text text text text text text text text text text
text text text text text text text text text text text
text text text text text text text text text text text
text text text text text text text text text text text
text text text text text text text text text text text
text text text text text text text text text text text
text text text text text text text text text text text
text text text text text text text text text text text
text text text text text text text text text text text

text text text text text text text text text text text
text text text text text text text text text text text
text text text text text text text text text text text
text text text text text text text text text text text
text text text text text text text text text text text
text text text text text text text text text text text
text text text text text text text text text text text
text text text text text text text text text text text
text text text text text text text text text text text
text text text text text text text text text text text
text text text text text text text text text text text
text text text text text text text text text text text
text text text text text text text text text text text
text text text text text text text text text text text
text text text text text text text text text text text
text text text text text text text text text text text
text text text text text text text text text text text
text text text text text text text text text text text
text text text text text text text text text text text
text text text text text text text text text text text
text text text text text text text text text text text
text text text text text text text text text text text
text text text text text text text text text text text
text text text text text text text text text text text
text text text text text text text text text text text
text text text text text text text text text text text
text text text text text text text text text text text
text text text text text text text text text text text
text text text text text text text text text text text
text text text text text text text text text text text
text text text text text text text text text text text
text text text text text text text text text text text
text text text text text text text text text text text
text text text text text text text text text text text
text text text text text text text text text text text
text text text text text text text text text text text

text text text text text text text text text text text
text text text text text text text text text text text
text text text text text text text text text text text
text text text text text text text text text text text
text text text text text text text text text text text
text text text text text text text text text text text
text text text text text text text text text text text
text text text text text text text text text text text
text text text text text text text text text text text
text text text text text text text text text text text
text text text text text text text text text text text
text text text text text text text text text text text
text text text text text text text text text text text
text text text text text text text text text text text
text text text text text text text text text text text
text text text text text text text text text text text
text text text text text text text text text text text
text text text text text text text text text text text
text text text text text text text text text text text
text text text text text text text text text text text
text text text text text text text text text text text
text text text text text text text text text text text
text text text text text text text text text text text
text text text text text text text text text text text
text text text text text text text text text text text
text text text text text text text text text text text
text text text text text text text text text text text
text text text text text text text text text text text
text text text text text text text text text text text
text text text text text text text text text text text
text text text text text text text text text text text
text text text text text text text text text text text
text text text text text text text text text text text
text text text text text text text text text text text
text text text text text text text text text text text
text text text text text text text text text text text
text text text text text text text text text text text

text text text text text text text text text text text
text text text text text text text text text text text
text text text text text text text text text text text
text text text text text text text text text text text
text text text text text text text text text text text
text text text text text text text text text text text
text text text text text text text text text text text
text text text text text text text text text text text
text text text text text text text text text text text
text text text text text text text text text text text
text text text text text text text text text text text
text text text text text text text text text text text
text text text text text text text text text text text
text text text text text text text text text text text
text text text text text text text text text text text
text text text text text text text text text text text
text text text text text text text text text text text
text text text text text text text text text text text
text text text text text text text text text text text
text text text text text text text text text text text
text text text text text text text text text text text
text text text text text text text text text text text
text text text text text text text text text text text
text text text text text text text text text text text
text text text text text text text text text text text
text text text text text text text text text text text
text text text text text text text text text text text
text text text text text text text text text text text
text text text text text text text text text text text
text text text text text text text text text text text
text text text text text text text text text text text
text text text text text text text text text text text
text text text text text text text text text text text
text text text text text text text text text text text
text text text text text text text text text text text

text text text text text text text text text text text
text text text text text text text text text text text
text text text text text text text text text text text
text text text text text text text text text text text
text text text text text text text text text text text
text text text text text text text text text text text
text text text text text text text text text text text
text text text text text text text text text text text
text text text text text text text text text text text
text text text text text text text text text text text
text text text text text text text text text text text
text text text text text text text text text text text
text text text text text text text text text text text
text text text text text text text text text text text
text text text text text text text text text text text
text text text text text text text text text text text
text text text text text text text text text text text
text text text text text text text text text text text
text text text text text text text text text text text
text text text text text text text text text text text
text text text text text text text text text text text
text text text text text text text text text text text
text text text text text text text text text text text
text text text text text text text text text text text
text text text text text text text text text text text
text text text text text text text text text text text
text text text text text text text text text text text
text text text text text text text text text text text
text text text text text text text text text text text
text text text text text text text text text text text
text text text text text text text text text text text
text text text text text text text text text text text
text text text text text text text text text text text
text text text text text text text text text text text
text text text text text text text text text text text
text text text text text text text text text text text

text text text text text text text text text text text
text text text text text text text text text text text
text text text text text text text text text text text
text text text text text text text text text text text
text text text text text text text text text text text
text text text text text text text text text text text
text text text text text text text text text text text
text text text text text text text text text text text
text text text text text text text text text text text
text text text text text text text text text text text
text text text text text text text text text text text
text text text text text text text text text text text
text text text text text text text text text text text
text text text text text text text text text text text
text text text text text text text text text text text
text text text text text text text text text text text
text text text text text text text text text text text
text text text text text text text text text text text
text text text text text text text text text text text
text text text text text text text text text text text
text text text text text text text text text text text
text text text text text text text text text text text
text text text text text text text text text text text
text text text text text text text text text text text
text text text text text text text text text text text
text text text text text text text text text text text
text text text text text text text text text text text
text text text text text text text text text text text
text text text text text text text text text text text
text text text text text text text text text text text
text text text text text text text text text text text
text text text text text text text text text text text
text text text text text text text text text text text
text text text text text text text text text text text
text text text text text text text text text text text
text text text text text text text text text text text
text text text text text text text text text text text

text text text text text text text text text text text
text text text text text text text text text text text
text text text text text text text text text text text
text text text text text text text text text text text
text text text text text text text text text text text
text text text text text text text text text text text
text text text text text text text text text text text

Acknowledgements

This book was written over the course of December and January of 2016 and 2017. I'd like to thank Olivia McCreary for her help editing this manuscript, Garrett Dennert for his dedication to my vision of the work and his help bringing this novel to life, Patty and Joe Corrao for their support throughout this process, Ari Newman, Summer Freed, and Joseph Wurm for tolerating me as I talked endlessly about the project, *decomP magazinE* who published the first chapter back in 2016, and lastly Man and Oh Man, who I've hated since the very beginning.

About Mike Corrao

Mike Corrao is a young writer and filmmaker working out of Minneapolis, where he earned his B.A. in film and English literature at the University of Minnesota. In 2016, he was an artist-in-residence for the Altered Esthetics Film Festival. His work has appeared in over 20 different publications, including *Entropy*, *decomP*, *Cleaver*, and the *Portland Review*.

Man, Oh Man is his first novel.

About Orson's Publishing

Orson's Publishing is an independent book publisher operating out of Seattle, Washington. Founded in 2016, Orson's delivers wise, yet approachable storytelling to readers everywhere. For more information, please visit orsonspublishing.com.